ALL THINGS DEADLY

(SALEM STORIES)

ERIK HANSON

D & T
PUBLISHING

CONTENTS

ACKNOWLEDGMENTS

I would like to thank the following people: Jonathan Maberry, Leah Franqui, Kendare Blake, Alan Gratz, Sandy Young, Robert Ottone, Robert Block, Steve DiUbaldo, Benjamin Gouldthorpe, Jennifer Tucker Nichols, Ruthann Jagge, Elizabeth Suggs, Derek Gray, Jared Andrews, and Emily Wachtel. Deepest gratitude, however, for my parents, who put up with my dark side. And, last but not least, my wife and daughter.

This book is for Dane

FOREWORD

This one surprised me. After devoting many of my post-college years to playwriting and screenwriting, I decided to try my hand at fiction. But why? Was this the result of my ego? Or was it the result of my curiosity? I would argue the latter; a select few in my life might suggest the former.

It's worth pointing out that I left Los Angeles after a two-year stint in 2004 to return to my home state of Connecticut. The announced goal was that I needed space to write my first novel. The underlying goal was to regain my sanity. Los Angeles and I didn't mix well. The final product ended up in a few composition notebooks. I don't remember the title or its contents. I never transferred it to a computer because I didn't think it contained much merit. Additionally, my handwriting is atrocious, which could have impacted my decision not to type and save it.

So, where did this collection come from? What were the steps that kicked this one into high gear? In chronological order, the following happened:

1. In the summer of 2019, I took a part-time job at a grocery store. More times than I can count, a co-worker encouraged me to visit Salem.

.

2.   After one visit to Salem, my wife and I fell in love with the place. We got married on the rooftop of a hotel in August 2020.

3.   COVID-19 kept going and going.

4.   While a screenwriting project remained in flux, I noticed how much the pandemic impacted the theatrical world. Some of my short plays went from the promise of being staged to a canceled production. A publisher that frequently inquired about my works lost his job. Fiction seemed less daunting.

5.   I outlined every single story in this book and thought that they might make a decent film anthology. But I soon realized that this was my way of remaining in the comfort zone. I needed to step out of it if I intended to grow as a writer.

6.   The Frost stories, or the main storyline, came about due to my brother's advice. He liked my outline but thought a frame would make the book seem a lot less random. I trusted his instincts. As a result, you have Adam and Sutton Frost.

Once I neared the end of my manuscript, I realized that I should start contacting people. I was beyond impressed by the level of support I received from the horror community. From established authors like the remarkable Jonathan Maberry to up-and-coming ones, they gave me sound advice. Without these replies to emails, I doubt I would be writing a foreword to anything. For this reason, I will pay it forward for others who want to take a crack at writing their first novel, collection, story, or drabble. Feel free to contact me, and I will do my best to assist you. That is, of course, if you like the contents.

All in all, this one isn't perfect. Some stories might end sooner than they should; others might be a little long in the tooth. Like a rookie in the big leagues, I took a big swing here. Whether readers think I struck out or hit a homer that eked its way over the fence isn't what's important. What's important is that I had a goal, stuck to it for nearly six months, and formed a final product. Will it lead to another book? I have no clue. I'm just happy that I did it. Whoever said "Happiness is in the doing" was dead on.

THE FROSTS—AN INTRODUCTION

IT WAS UNUSUALLY warm for a Connecticut day in October. The sweat built up on Adam Frost's bald head, causing him to drive with one hand on the wheel and the other on a fast-food napkin. His daughter, Sutton, sat in the passenger seat. The only communication from her came in the form of harsh glances. One glance towards the A/C that didn't work. Another glance at her father dabbing his wet head. A final glance out the window suggesting she would rather be anywhere but with the man who helped create her.

Adam checked the clock. They departed their home thirty-eight minutes ago, and, as it stood, his daughter hadn't made a verbal peep. He dared to offer a few remarks about his job (stocking groceries and building displays), his new favorite show about transsexual zombies, and his opinion on the leaves displaying color combinations he had never witnessed in New England. Sutton didn't just meet every one of his remarks with silence; she met them with body posture that announced her reluctance to speak about anything at all. Adam was yet to try questions. Surely those guaranteed responses?

"Aren't you warm?"

Nothing.

"Isn't that sweatshirt too heavy?

Nothing.

"It would feel heavy on me. Don't you want to take it off?"

"I'm. Fine."

Adam knew she wasn't, but he had no clue how to bridge the verbal gap. He didn't care that she was wearing an oversized hoodie; he cared about what the hoodie was covering: cuts along her arms.

Adam hit a considerable amount of traffic. During the wait, he studied his daughter intently. Her sandy brown hair hung over her face like a shield. He wanted to lift her bangs and scream in her face, "What's wrong?!" But he didn't do that. Instead, he adjusted the dial on the thermostat, which produced next to no cold air. He looked left and right. A tractor-trailer with gargantuan wheels passed by his door. An electric car inched past Sutton's side, with a hula dancer figurine dangling off the antenna. He directed her attention to it. She stared back blankly.

He returned his attention to the road, fearing that their destination could exacerbate her internal pain instead of providing the cure.

DRIPS

BILLY HATED living at The Gardens. He hated the faux brick on the building's exterior and the moldy walls on its interior. The lime green carpeting that covered floors 1 and 2 made him sick; the popcorn ceilings appeared as if they would burst at any second. He wondered if kernels were hidden in there, too.

He blamed his mother for it. Had she been able to find a decent man, she wouldn't be on the run, continuously shuffling apartments here and there. Unfortunately, the apartments were identical to the men: they kept getting worse. Even though Billy detested his new home, he dreaded the thought of ending up in a place worse than The Gardens. He didn't want to believe that it was possible, but he had seen the other end of it. He had to thank his mother's frequent swings and misses for that.

The only bright spot for the nearly eleven-year-old Billy was that Halloween was here. In a few hours, he would be able to snag as much candy as possible. His only concern—the only variable in the candy-snagging operation—was when he started. If Billy wasn't the early bird, he ran the risk of acquiring next to nothing. And his mother wouldn't care. She never even put out candy!

He started on the second floor. Much to his surprise, there were plenty of buckets and dishes left out for trick-or-treaters. He thought about removing his werewolf mask because no one would play witness to his costume if all the tenants' doors remained closed. Then again, he thought he would come across as a thief if he cruised down the hall with nothing on but his regular hand-me-down clothes. In addition to meeting the requirements of a Halloween costume, Billy's mask served another purpose. It helped counter the pot smell that was emanating from the walls. Yes, he was familiar with pot. His brain triggered a flashback from three years ago. He tossed and turned in bed. He sat up, realizing that a funky smell was the reason he snapped out of deep sleep. He slipped out of bed, hoping to inform his mother that their apartment had been infused with poison and that they had to leave ASAP. But when he reached her bedroom, he found his mother inhaling a smoky substance from what he'd later learn was a bong. Pot was her major vice, and Billy wished she would quit it altogether.

Billy moved swiftly down the hall. Before he started the candy haul, he mapped out the following strategy in his head: he would bend down, take a small handful from each basket or bowl, offer a loud "Thank you" to the unseen providers (whether they were home or not), and then repeat until he reached the end of the hallway. If he took too much candy by accident, he would drop a piece or two back. It was only fair.

It took him less than a minute to complete the run. Of the twelve units on the floor, seven tenants had put out candy. He began his descent down the stairwell when a voice suddenly greeted him from behind.

"Where do you think you're going?"

He didn't like the person's tone, but it didn't stop him from returning to the upstairs hallway.

"I do something wrong?"

"You didn't knock on my door and ask for candy."

"Do you want me to?"

The tenant backed into his apartment and slammed the door shut. Billy was taken aback by the man's jarring action. He considered leaving, but he knocked on the door instead. The door opened and a clown answered.

"Trick or—"

"Close your eyes."

For no other reason than the man having an enormous bowl of candy, Billy complied with the man's order. He closed his eyes and waited, standing frighteningly still. A lump of significant weight landed in Billy's pillowcase.

"Am I done?"

"Are you done?" the clown asked in a challenging tone.

"I can have more?"

"I don't know, can you?"

"I don't think I need more."

"All kids need more."

"Okay."

"Keep those eyes closed and say please."

"Please?"

Billy's pillowcase nearly fell to the floor. It was official: he wouldn't need to visit the first floor.

"Thank you very much, Sir."

Just like moments ago, the door slammed in Billy's face. He took a deep breath and bolted towards the stairwell. Had he not been looking down at the bulky shape in his pillowcase, he would have seen the tall vampire in front of him and pivoted at the last second. Unfortunately for Billy, it was a direct hit. The vampire screamed, "What the hell, bruh!" as he went back to the middle landing. Billy landed on top of him with a loud thunk. The vampire, his fangs on the dirty floor, shoved Billy off with clenched fists.

Billy's head was ringing. He struggled to get the mask off. As the piece of plastic tore away from his face, he saw stars where the walls should be. He was vaguely aware of the vampire stuffing candy into his pillowcase.

"You don't have to do that," Billy said.

"You're right. I don't."

The vampire stood, walked up the stairwell, and vanished from sight. Billy glanced at the floor. Candy was everywhere! In between a package of Starburst and Reese's Pieces was a keychain. A miniature llama dangled off the end, wearing a shirt that read "No Prob-Llama." Billy chuckled. He stuffed all he could into his pillowcase and hauled tail to his apartment.

The door was open a crack, which made Billy take pause. His mother was one of those "excessive lockers," meaning that she would lock the door and then put the chain up as well. It annoyed Billy daily when he had to beg his mother to enter his place of living. That said, he understood that she was afraid of bad men—a handful of the ones she dated—who all but guaranteed that she would get hers if they ever discovered where she was living. Billy remembered a few threats. One ex promised to tear her apart limb from the limb; another swore to get revenge on her for breaking his heart in two.

Thinking it had more to do with the holiday than any safety issue, Billy dragged the pillowcase to his bedroom and shut the door. A gross apartment complex or not, this haul of his was epic. He sat on his Minecraft comforter, tilted the pillowcase, and watched his candy fall out.

Billy's mood shifted from glee to horror. The amount of Snickers didn't matter; the amount of Twix didn't matter; the amount of Butterfingers didn't matter; the amount of Three Musketeers didn't matter; the amount of candy combined didn't matter. Why? Because lying in the middle of his candy haul was something that would make him seek his mother's comfort immediately: a bloody knife.

"Mom?"

No response. Billy raised his voice.

"Mom?!"

Still nothing. Billy's only reluctance for yelling louder was because his mother hated it. Whenever she would call on him for an errand or to inform him that yet another TV dinner was ready, he would reply with "What?" in a volume that made her visibly cringe.

Billy looked at his shaking hands. This event skyrocketed to number one on his life experience list. Did the knife belong to the bizarre clown? Had he snuck it in there? Or was it the douchey vampire? Whose blood was it? Was it real or fake blood?

The Salem Police would be in charge of answering those questions. All Billy had to do was tell his mother. She would know what to do since her life experience list was a lot more varied and colorful than Billy's.

As if it were a crime scene, Billy sidestepped the candy and slithered out of the room. He walked down the short hallway and turned into the living room. The TV was blaring. In tandem with the TV volume, a teakettle whistled with all its might from the kitchen. The unusual bit about both wasn't that they were happening in unison; it was that they were happening at all. Billy's mother disliked loud noises, and he reckoned that she hated the flavor of tea more.

Billy muted the TV and planned on doing the same for the teakettle. But that would require him to completely ignore the fact that his mother, the serial dater without a clue or college degree, was wailing in pain in the middle of the kitchen floor.

The amount of blood shocked Billy. He noticed three large slash marks on her body: one across her chest, a second in her stomach, and a third right below the neck. His mother applied pressure to this area, but the blood had a mind of its own.

"What should I do?" Billy asked, doubtful that there was any solution.

Blood gargled in his mother's mouth. Instead of using words and wasting the little energy she had left, she pointed to the house phone mounted near the microwave wall. Billy stepped forward, lifted the receiver off the base, and dialed 9. Then 1.

Suddenly, it dawned on Billy. The bloody knife was still in his room. He could get rid of it. Or he could leave it where it was and allow whichever policeman that arrived at the scene to discover it. He knew that this was a risky move since he would become the first and only suspect.

His mother kept pointing to the phone. Sweat poured down Billy's forehead. It wasn't even hot out. But this was one pressure-cooker of a moment. Billy closed his eyes and counted to five.

"One...two...three...four...five!"

Instead of calling 911, instead of booking it towards his bedroom to retrieve the knife, Billy ran out of the apartment as fast as possible. He passed an elderly couple on the way out. Did he inform them of the random attack on his mother? No, he did not. He kept on running and running and running.

LAST BREATHS

HENRY AWOKE and stared at the clock. It was three past nine in the morning. This Salem hotel must have special powers because he had never slept past seven in nearly a decade. The one instance when he did, had been the result of a happy hour run amok.

There was a commotion coming from the streets below. *So much for the hotel having special powers*, thought Henry.

He swayed on his feet and entered the chic bathroom. He checked himself out in the mirror. He was tousle-haired. Social media would get a kick out of this particular look if he had an account on any of the popular sites.

He splashed water on his face and then tapped his cheeks. He had done this routine since he was a child and had no intention of stopping unless a beautiful love interest, of which there was none, ordered him to break the habit.

He lowered his flower-print boxers and took a leak. "Oh no!" he yelled when his first stream of urine hit the seat and traveled towards the back wall. Even with no one watching, this embarrassed him. He altered his unit's angle and focused hard on the circular hole at the bottom of the toilet.

He flushed the toilet and raised his boxers. A few drops of urine trickled out of his pecker. His shame was real. Women didn't understand the difficulty of being a man. Then and there, he considered sitting on the toilet from that moment on. His mess rate would decrease monumentally.

Sirens blared outside. Henry still paid it no mind. He expected it to end in less than a minute. He climbed back into bed, grabbed his cell phone off the nightstand, and unlocked it. No messages.

He turned on the TV to counter the loud noises outside. He assumed Salem was just a chaotic place. He flipped through a few channels: the local news, a documentary about Egyptian pyramids, and then a sports highlight show. Nothing attracted his interest.

He had brought *A Collection of Essays* by George Orwell with him. Powering off the TV, he decided to read that while he waited for his job interview later that day. He was overly curious to find out what Orwell thought about Charles Dickens. He slipped out of bed and headed towards the desk where his backpack sat. He opened it up and dug around. The book wasn't there. He had forgotten to pack it.

With nothing to distract him but the exterior noise, Henry moved towards the window. The blinds, all of which were a mishmash of Navajo designs and contemporary flair, were down. He grabbed the white chain along the left side and paused. It wasn't evident whether he should pull down or guide it upward. He went with the latter. Nothing happened. When he realized that pulling it down would force the blind to go up, it was too late. A piece of the white chain ripped off the wall.

Henry sat on the gray couch. He considered calling the front desk to inform them about the damage. He waited. He dropped the notion of a call; instead, he would take the elevator down to tell them face-to-face. A little interaction never hurt anybody, and Henry was the type that could benefit from social activity.

Henry grabbed his keycards, shoved them into the hotel's envelope, and headed towards the elevator. The elevator, according to a hurried scribble on pink paper, was out of order. Huffing, he traced his way to the stairwell.

Henry made it to the front desk two minutes later. To his surprise, no one was there. The office behind the check-in desk was devoid of beings, too. He walked around the corner, towards the entrance doors, assuming that someone, any member of staff, would be in the kitchen area that had been closed down since COVID-19 wreaked havoc on the minds and bodies of the nation.

Henry glanced outside. There was no one out there. But the raucous noise spoke to the contrary. He pushed through the glass doors and stepped onto the brick-lined path.

A voice boomed in the distance. "Nice shirt, pal!"

Henry peered down at his t-shirt. He wasn't sure the message was directed at him until the voice continued.

"You bet your bottom black lives matter!"

Henry smirked. Born to a white mother and black father, he grew up without getting involved in racial matters. But as time wore on, his lighter skin made others assume that he was white and white only.

This sweeping generalization made by teachers, bosses, friends, and acquaintances became so tiresome that he started to open his usually shut mouth.

His most recent job interview at a prep school in Connecticut was a turning point. As he neared the end of a lengthy question session about a History vacancy, Henry was asked, point-blank, by the principal, what separated him from all of the other candidates.

"For starters, I am black *and* white. It gives me a leg up on others in my understanding of racial matters."

The six bodies interviewing him turned awkward. Instead of jotting down a note about his response, the principal responded with one question:

"You're really black?"

Henry knew he could have filed a grievance with the school. He opted against it and decided to play the long game. He applied to jobs in Massachusetts. Salem was the first area that showed interest.

Henry made his way down Essex Street. He had left his tortoise-shell glasses in his room. He didn't need them to process this chaotic scene.

White people of all genders and ages protested that their lives mattered and that there would be a reckoning. The local cops, all of whom were black, taunted them back. Henry couldn't believe his eyes and ears.

Henry kept walking down Essex Street. An elderly white woman tossed a Molotov cocktail into a business that supported blacks. Two cops arrested her in seconds. A white homeless man begged a black female cop for a dollar. When she said no, he whipped a knife out and told her that her life was worthless. She knocked him out with her baton. A soccer mom went into attack mode after a black hostess denied her entrance into a café that had the best cappuccinos in town. A seasoned cop, with salt and pepper hair and mustache, did his best to intervene. But it was too late. The white business owner appeared and poured a hot cup of cappuccino all over the soccer mom's heavily made-up face. The woman screamed like a banshee.

The aggression ramped up. Henry needed to find cover. Even

though he didn't have his glasses' assistance, he located a patisserie that was vacant minus a black barista who sported a yellow hoodie with Malcolm X's face on it. Before he reached the entrance door, he eluded a white yuppie. Said yuppie stood inches away from a burly black cop. He delivered a rant that, if heard, would have secured him a job on the Fox News network.

Henry slipped into the patisserie. He approached the barista, whose warm smile suggested she was beyond fine with everything that was occurring in the city today. His mouth watered at all of the dessert options. Since childhood, he had a sweet tooth that was yet another habit he had no intention of stopping unless a beautiful love interest ordered him to do so. The barista would have been a contender if she were a tad older.

Feeling pressured to order something even though no one waited behind him, Henry shifted the power over to the barista.

"Tell you what: I'll take a dozen of the macarons. You pick the flavors."

The barista grabbed a rectangular box and slid a collection of flaw-less-looking sweets into the box. Henry checked the scene outside. He couldn't make out the actual dialogue, but the yuppie dared the black cop to strike him.

Henry collected his macarons, dropped a twenty-dollar bill into the tip jar, and grabbed a seat in front of the glass window. The yuppie smirked at Henry as if they were cut from the same cloth. Henry stared at him to convey that they weren't. Enraged, the yuppie delivered the "n-word" and head-butted the cop. Instantly, the cop spun him around and body-slammed him on the concrete. Henry stood with his mouth agape. He couldn't help but identify with the cop's impulse.

The burly cop bent down and directed his knee at the yuppie's vulnerable neck. But then he made eyes with Henry and pulled back. They shared a knowing nod. The cop turned back, and pressed the cussing yuppie against the storefront window, handcuffing him.

Henry was suddenly aware of the barista mumbling behind him.

"What the eff? I thought he was gonna crush that racist's neck."

Henry smirked.

"Come on. You know we don't do that."

The barista returned to her station, still mumbling under her breath. Henry's eyes followed the cop as he led the still-cussing yuppie to his cruiser. He then opened his box of macarons, and, one by one, ate them feeling more satisfied than he had ever been in his twenty-six-year existence.

ZUKES

IT WAS Jason's first job. He would have quit less than eight minutes into shift number one if his stepfather didn't run the cinema. He didn't know how to describe his job role other than to say that he was the building's utility player.

Rip tickets? Yep, he did it.

Work the concession stand? Yep, he did it.

Sweep the floors of every theater? Yep, he did it.

Spray and wipe down the piss and crap left behind in bathrooms? Yep, he did it.

Most of his friends had the luxury of playing their parents for fools by pretending to search and apply for jobs. Not Jason. His stepfather was a real slave driver, and his mother—who once had a mind and opinions of her own—had become a slave to the workaholic she married.

Jason's interview took place in the kitchen four nights ago.

"I need help at the cinema."

Instead of giving his stepfather a verbal response, Jason went with the eyebrow raise and half-smirk combo.

"I need *you* to help me at the cinema."

"He needs help," his mother added, as she put down a bowl of mayonnaise-free potato salad.

"My hearing is fully functional," said Jason.

"Don't get fresh."

"I'm not being—"

His stepfather pointed the potato salad spoon like a surly judge with a gavel.

"You'll start tomorrow. I need help every day but Sundays and Mondays. Do what you want on your free days. But you're mine on the others. We're getting a big movie tomorrow, so it's all hands on deck."

"She helping too?"

"I'm 43 years old!" his mother guffawed.

"Which makes you too old or too young?"

"I'm not working at a cinema."

"He said all hands-on—"

"Eat your food, and shut up."

"Apologize, and I'll work for him."

Jason wanted to hold to his demand, but he surrendered like most teenagers who foolishly confront their parents. He went to the cinema the next night.

Why he wanted to quit in eight minutes had nothing to do with the menial tasks assigned to him; it had everything to do with the behavior of the patrons. He would attest that various films made him excited; however, he had seen nothing like this in all his days growing up in Salem. Women and men—mostly women though—were excited. Some would drop their torn ticket after Jason handed it back; some would howl in the lobby as if they had just discovered fresh prey hiding in the building; some would speak slightly above a whisper, ashamed that they were going to see this film; some would push and shove past the others to get the best available seats.

And what was the film?

Hot Hot Hot was an erotica novel self-published by Allyson O'Malley, a woman that had been divorced six times. The number of divorces made her an expert on all things sexual. At least that is what she claimed in the foreword. Critics panned the novel at the outset. Few found any redeeming qualities with the character, dialogue, or story. But in the evolving days of social media, the author convinced most of her Twitter followers to purchase the book. Said convincing occurred via mini-posts that included steamy excerpts. The content was so rich with passion that those who took the bait had to discover what would happen next. This brilliant tactic—one had to concede it was intelligent even if they thought she had no business in the creative field—led to sale after sale.

Jason didn't understand it. Sure, he understood, as much as it pained him, that people his parents' age thought about sex too. He could not, however, wrap his brain around people rushing to see a rated R film. There was a story written in one of the national papers that suggested the film should be given the NC-17 rating. Regardless, a movie about one middle-aged woman's affairs with multiple men seemed downright boring.

Before the credits began in the first showing at the cinema, Jason could hear a cacophony of chatter with harsh tones. Speaking of harsh tones, a woman of nearly sixty years turned to Jason as he examined whether or not there was an empty seat in the place.

"Are you gonna just stand there?"

"If I do?" Jason asked.

"People spent big money to see this."

"This movie doesn't cost more than any of the others playing here."

"Toodle-oo!"

Jason wanted to go off. He tried to ruin the moviegoing experience for her and others. But he was disarmed because he was given the toodle-oo for the first time in his life.

Mere minutes later, Jason attempted to fix the popcorn machine because, according to his stepdad, it had stopped making popcorn.

"I don't think it's a machine problem. I think it's an electrical problem."

"Fix it then," his stepfather barked.

"I'm not an electrician."

"I cannot have zero popcorn for the opening night of the biggest movie in, um, decades."

Before Jason could challenge this film's importance, his stepfather ran off to resolve a line dispute. Without his stepfather's eyes on him, Jason grabbed the machine's plug rather spontaneously and looked at the clerk with vintage glasses and multi-colored hair. She stared at him and then the plug. He removed it from the wall outlet. The machine whirred for thirty seconds, before going lifeless.

"What's that look about? It wasn't popping. How could this hurt?"

Jason hoped the girl would be taken by his gesture, or at the very least, deliver him a smile. All she did was shrug. The machine roared back to life, and the popcorn resumed popping. Jason locked eyes with the clerk. She smiled.

Feeling like he was on top of the world, Jason cruised towards the men's room to check its condition. While the place was mostly spotless, there were a few receipts on the floor. Jason tossed them out, not for once considering their importance.

The volume reached an epic level in Cinema 1. Based on his previous encounter with a woman and the patrons' general vibe altogether, Jason knew it would be frowned upon if he entered the theater while the movie was knee-deep in the middle of the narrative. But he had never heard such reactions.

Regardless, he decided to turn his attention to the women's room.

"Hello? Anybody in there?"

No responses allowed Jason to do a quick sweep of the area. Like the men's room, the place was clean, save receipts, and a handful of shredded plastic sleeves that appeared to have been wrapped around some vegetables.

This factor made Jason check the receipts. All of them confirmed purchases of a single item from the produce department. This perplexed Jason. He would surely understand patrons sneaking in candy or booze or some snack from home to save money. But why were they purchasing the vegetable listed on the receipts?

A disturbing thought crossed Jason's mind. He shook his head. There was no way.

Jason entered Cinema 1 and walked less than twenty yards across the carpeted hallway when he witnessed the aforementioned vegetable's real purpose. He swore in disbelief, covered his eyes, and then rushed out of the theater.

Jason found his stepfather adjusting the framed poster of *Hot Hot Hot*.

"I need to speak with you."

"This isn't a time for speaking; it's a time for working."

"I need a minute NOW!"

His stepfather could put up with Jason's snarky comebacks. He could put up with his unhygienic nature. He could put up with his average grades in school. He could not, however, put up with being yelled at in his own business.

"In my office."

Jason knew he was in for it. But what he had to share was so crucial that he would endure a verbal blasting.

"If you ever raise your voice to me in MY business, so help me God, I'll—"

"You have to shut the theater down. ASAP."

"Shut it down? Did you see the number of people here tonight? Have you seen how far the line goes outside? It wraps around the building and goes all the way to the Essex Oyster Bar."

"I get it, but…"

"No, you don't get it. This is going to bring us in so much money."

"Forget the money. This is absurd."

"Making money is absurd?"

"Their behavior is."

"And you're the expert on behavior? You treat your mother like dirt. You do the same with your teachers. You barely have any friends. You haven't had a girlfriend yet. And all that is okay, but you might want to consider how your daily behavior prevents you from having success in that particular category."

"This isn't about me."

"I wouldn't be away from the floor for a second if it wasn't for you."

"All I ask…"

"No."

"If you don't do what I ask, I'll quit."

"This place has been long successful without you as an employee. I'll replace you quickly."

"Nobody will want to have my job when they see what's happening in that theater."

"Nothing's going on in my theater."

"You don't have to pay me for my shift. I beg you. Please take a walk with me inside Cinema 1."

"After I do so, you're going to work your little tail off until closing time, and your efforts are going to be free of charge."

"It's a deal."

Jason couldn't believe he had convinced his stepfather to go in there. He half-expected one of two things to happen: his stepfather would fire him on the spot and not do what he asked, or he would get his stepfather in there, and nothing would be amiss. Like it was something taken from *The Twilight Zone*.

This is why Jason led the way. He felt like a young detective aiming to prove his superior wrong. Jason opened the doors to Cinema 1; his stepfather followed with a "let's get this nonsense over with" energy. Jason stopped at the end of the mini-hallway, which is where the stadium seating started. He peeked into the crowd and let out a massive sigh of relief.

His stepfather tried to take in the scene. His mouth opened, but no words came out.

"Have you ever seen anything like this?"

His stepfather thought of all the dramatic moments that occurred over the sixteen years of his ownership. A woman had a heart attack while watching an animated movie with her grandkids; a man battling Alzheimer's had to be restrained for threatening all of the customers because he thought they were fighting on the side of Vietnam; a teenager showed up in a black trench coat and pretended to shoot up the place. While the kid was arrested, he wouldn't be locked away forever since the weapon was no more than a water pistol painted black.

"Call...the...cops."

"For real? This a police matter?" Jason asked.

"It's a moral matter, and I cannot think of anyone else to call. Can you?"

Jason checked his cell. No service. He ran out of the theater and stopped in the middle of the lobby. Still no bars. He made a break for the parking lot.

Meanwhile, his stepfather watched in horror as his paying viewers put smooth zucchinis inside every orifice available to them. Some did it alone. Some did it with others. Some watched while they eagerly waited their turn. Some fought each other because they had abused their vegetable too much. Some talked about how the zucchini was a vegetable to be adored instead of abused.

In the middle of the parking lot, Jason finally got a signal. He dialed 911. When a raspy female voice asked him the nature of the emergency, he, in a rushed breath, said, "You have to see it to believe it."

THE FIVE-DAY FISHERMAN

MONDAY

THE MAN DIDN'T RECALL how or why he had come to Gloucester; the only thing that concerned him was catching fish. He didn't do it for money but the thrill.

His apartment (*living space* would be a more accurate descriptor), existed above a bait and tackle shop frequented by the likes of the young and old, the kind and rude, the pauperized, and the prosperous. The room consisted of a double bed, Navajo blanket, wooden chair, bearskin rug ruined by cigarette burns, steel waste bin, and a lamp in the shape of a lighthouse.

He woke daily at seven in the morning—courtesy of his human alarm clock. Even though her radiant charm bracelet announced her name (Emma) to the world, the man strictly referred to her as *the girl*.

"Time to get up."

"Who says?"

"Me says."

She picked an empty bottle of rum off the floor, shook her head with disapproval, and dropped it into the waste bin.

"You drink too much."

"You talk too much."

"Fishin' today?"

"I fish every day."

The man slipped out of bed and wiped his eyes.

"You got crust near your lips too," the girl pointed out.

The man studied her innocent expression. Had an adult said this, he would have replied with a snarky remark.

"Off you go."

"The sea is your oyster."

"The saying is…"

She cut him off here.

"I know the saying!"

He laughed. She laughed. He waved her away. She hesitated to comply with his nonverbal demand.

.

"Gotta get changed now. Don't need the authorities arresting me for indecency around a minor."

"Catch me a big bass."

"I'll catch what I catch."

Emma, or *the girl* rather, left his living space and ventured down a spiral staircase. The man peeked into the waste bin and removed the bottle. The girl was wrong to dispose of it. There was a bit of dark rum left. He unscrewed the cap and tilted the bottle; a few drops of the sweet stuff kissed his chapped lips.

TUESDAY

Unlike the day before, the bottle never made it to the floor.

Emma pried a bottle of silver rum from the man's grasp. All of this occurred while his eyes remained closed.

"Leave it be," the man warned.

"Time. To. Get. Up."

"Who says?"

"Me says."

The man opened his eyes, located the girl's warm yet no-nonsense face, and sat up.

"Catch anything yesterday?"

"Nuthin'."

"Probly catch something if you didn't have a bottle of *this* in you."

"The one don't impact the other."

"I disagree."

"That's yer right."

The man nudged her off his bed. He tossed his empty bottle into the waste bin and then snagged a shirt and work pants off the nearby chair.

"You know the drill."

"How come you never catch any fish?"

The man processed the question. He had no truth to give her. He had no lie to give her either.

"Move along."

"Catch me a big trout."

"I'll catch what I catch."

She winked at him, knowing that he would most likely catch nothing. Before she left, she turned back in the doorway.

"I go out fishing with you sometime?"

"Never."

"Just like that?"

"Just like it. Vamoose, little lady."

"Vamoose, old man."

He laughed. She laughed. He waved her away. She complied with his nonverbal demand.

He put on a t-shirt, slacks, and socks that hadn't been washed in days. It didn't matter if he smelled good around a bunch of fish.

WEDNESDAY

Emma stared at him while he snored. His worn face had so many wrinkles that if one took a blue pen to his face and outlined them, it would replicate a series of rivers.

He rolled over on his side and arranged the pillow to his liking. The girl marveled at the fact that he was still asleep. He licked his lips. She sneezed. He opened his eyes.

"Bless you."

"And also you."

He scooted off the bed—this time fully dressed. The girl appreciated him being fully clothed but failed to have the same opinion about the pungent smell wafting from his wiry frame. She didn't know which was preferable: shirtless or stinky?

"Catch anything yesterday?"

His face provided the answer. The girl frowned.

"Know what I think?"

"Nope."

"Want some of my advice?"

"I most definitely do not."

The man ignored her. The girl held her words back for as long as she possibly could.

"You need to take me out on your boat."

"Bad idea."

"Good idea."

"Kids ain't allowed."

"On all boats or just yours?"

"Mine."

"I know how to catch the fish."

"I am sure you believe that."

The girl made her way to the door, knowing that her time was about up. It dawned on her that he didn't fall asleep with a bottle or that one fell out of his hands in the night. This perked up her mood. Perhaps a transformation was on the man's horizon. But as the optimistic thought swirled around her brain, she spotted two empty smaller bottles that would equal his normal-sized one, on the bearskin rug.

"The booze ain't worth it."

"You're nine. What do you know what's worth it?"

"I know the booze ain't worth it."

The girl left his living space without wishing him luck or asking him to catch her a fish. Hungover or not, the man noticed these verbal omissions from their daily dialogue, and it, believe it or not, unnerved him.

THURSDAY

By some miracle, the man did two shocking things: he woke up without his human alarm and went a single evening without alcohol.

The man felt a certain emptiness that was devoid of explanation. He didn't know why either event happened. Well, that wasn't technically true. He had no clue why the girl didn't show up that morning, but he had every clue why he didn't drink booze the night before. The girl got under his skin with her omissions.

He was under the impression that if he went a night without the alcohol, she, the girl, would be proud of him and, therefore, think of him as less of a ne'er-do-well.

Not only did the man not fish this particular day, but he did not even leave his living space.

The day took forever to pass. The man, generally reserved of emotion, did not like it. At all.

FRIDAY

He didn't recall how or why he had arrived in Salem. The only thing that concerned him was the girl's whereabouts.

His room (*living space* would be a more accurate descriptor), did not exist above a bait and tackle shop. Instead, it existed above a shop devoted to penny candy. Obnoxious children and their bossy grand-mothers mostly frequented it. The room consisted of a double bed, Navajo blanket, wooden chair, bearskin rug ruined by cigarette burns, steel waste bin, and a lamp in the shape of a lighthouse. This puzzled him. The accuracy of it. The layout was exactly like his place in Gloucester.

Where was the girl? Unlike most mysteries, he solved it relatively fast.

He stopped in front of a full-length mirror and studied the being before him. He didn't look anything like the man in Gloucester. Because he wasn't the man from Gloucester.

The man spotted an unopened bottle of rum near his bay window. When he picked it up, he paused. It wasn't to check out the type of rum or to reconsider consuming it. Oh no. His eyes latched on to a picture tacked to the cobwebbed wall. Two figures in the grainy picture were recognizable. It was a younger version of himself and a young girl. His girl. He removed the picture from the wall and flipped it over. There was a single caption written in red ink:

"Gloucester Days. 2016."

The man tacked the picture back onto the wall. A daddy longlegs scurried up past his hand. His eyes noticed a few newspaper clippings. They read:

"Mystery at Sea,"
"Accident or foul play?"
"Is the father to blame?"

Only the man could answer the questions posed by the second and third clippings. A million thoughts raced through his mind. The one that wouldn't go away, despite all mental efforts, was that he was not a fisherman. He was never a fisherman. He was a realtor who purchased a boat to impress a daughter that was being taken away from him in an ugly custody battle. "It'll be a lovely day at sea," he promised his ex. She didn't care about it being lovely. She cared about him not drinking. He had promised that, too.

Yes, he sometimes missed his ex-wife. But he missed Emma so much more. She was his reason for working. She was his reason for breathing. She was his only reason.

"Is the father to blame?" he asked. He stood in this moment and lived in it for what felt like years. Scrambled images hit him like bullets. Emma tripping. The splashing waters. Emma screaming for help. The boat wobbling. Instead of answering the question for an empty room, he grabbed the bottle of rum, unscrewed the cap, and drank it all in one goddamn go.

ADAM FROST

EVERYONE THOUGHT he was a good father. And yet, had Adam Frost pulled back the curtain and revealed the truth, they would have noticed his high level of incompetence.

The events of the past decade eroded every ounce of his parental confidence. Raising a female teenager with a partner was difficult; raising a female teenager alone was nearly impossible.

He noticed the scratches on Sutton's wrists four days ago.

He wanted to freak out. But communicating with Sutton about anything was like playing a game of Russian roulette. The results of his encounters always felt like he earned, and maybe deserved, the bullet.

As he entertained the prospect of sending her to a facility to address whatever concerns were brewing inside her, he received a call from an old friend.

"You picked up!"

Terry Dennis, the caller, was a childhood friend and former business partner. He didn't call unless he wanted something.

"What do you want?" Adam asked.

"Nothing other than to wish you a Happy Birthday."

Adam wished Terry didn't acknowledge the fact that he was officially one year older. His daughter hadn't said a word to him, hadn't posted anything on social media, hadn't left a card for him to find. This made the day worthless. Terry's acknowledgment was like tossing salt on an already deep wound.

"How old are you now? 71?"

Terry's sense of humor never failed to irk Adam. Everything was a joke in Terry's eyes; everything was a disaster in Adam's.

"What. Do. You. Want."

"Busy next week?" Terry wondered.

"Extremely."

"Working? Dating? Lounging? Hanging with the daw-ta?"

"All of those."

"I refuse to accept any of those answers. Seriously, I don't."

"Won't change anything."

"I need you. You need me. Your daughter needs—"

"Don't act like you know what my daughter needs," Adam warned.

Adam detested when Terry made remarks like this. Sure, Terry knew the Frost family's whole sordid history, but it didn't give him the right to claim what Sutton needed in her life. That was for Adam to find out and Adam only.

"Overstepped my bounds. I am backing up now. Beep-beep-beep. Okay. Just ask me one question."

Adam groaned. "What?"

"That's not the question I want you to ask."

"What would you like me to ask?"

"Ask where my next assignment is," Terry teased.

Adam hated social games. He preferred when people shot him straight. But his current option was hanging up and living in the silence of his pathetic birthday.

"Where is your n—"

"Salem!"

Terry interrupted everyone. People scolded him all the time for this flaw, but it was a moot point. Bringing it up meant he would interrupt twice as much.

"No reaction to that location? None? Really? Okay. Ask me the address of the home with all of the spooky activity."

"Will you hang up when I do?"

"Most likely."

"What's the address?"

"171 Piedmont."

Adam hung up. The phone rang a second later. He gulped a full glass of water before answering.

"What now?"

"I was supposed to do the hanging up!"

Adam filled another glass of water. This was too much to process. He wished Terry didn't bother him, let alone with news like this. But he couldn't blame the guy for keeping him abreast of this paranormal development. The location carried too much relevance.

"I need you."

"You think I'd actually go on camera again and—"

"No cameras. We're not making an episode about it. Out of respect."

"That's...kind."

"I know it is! My team wanted to film there. One of the producers practically ordered me to. But I stood up to all of 'em."

"I haven't been to Salem in—"

"Nine years to be exact. I counted. You don't have to give me an answer this second. The morning is fine."

"My answer is no."

"Would Sutton's answer be no?"

"She would never say yes. She hates Salem."

"Because you programmed her to hate it."

Terry had a point. Still, Adam had more pressing matters than visiting a familiar house three hours away. He had to confront his daughter and find out why the cuts on her arms were expanding daily.

"I'll ask, but I won't pressure her."

"Understood. Last thing. Going to play some audio for you."

"Please don't."

"Shush! Now listen."

Adam pressed his ear against the phone. The audio crackled and hissed. It seemed like no clarity was in sight. Then he heard it. Muffled words. Two of them.

"Well?" Terry asked.

"Hard to make out."

"You're lying to me, and you're lying to yourself!"

Adam was lying. Terry didn't need to see an expression to know it either. He knew Adam like the back of his hand.

"*Let her.*"

"It doesn't say that."

"It does too! I've had, like, seventeen friends back me up on this."

"You know how many things sound like that? Let her? Get her. Met her. Set her. Bet her."

"Pretend for a second that I'm right," Terry said.

Adam allowed himself to see Terry's point of view. His Sutton problem didn't go away with this unsubstantial data, however.

With a hint of optimism, Terry said, "This could change things between the two of you."

At that, Adam hung up again. He ignored the calls and texts that followed. He sat down at the kitchen table. He hated when Terry offered parenting advice. Terry had no kids, no wife, few friends, and parents that stopped talking to him the second he graduated high school to announce he was going to become a ghost hunter. Regardless of these facts, Adam believed that Terry was right.

A floorboard creaked in the hall. As Sutton appeared, Adam was filled with hope. Perhaps she, before committing to bedtime, remembered the importance of this day and was ready to deliver the two words that everyone receives for reaching another age milestone.

"You got a paperclip?"

For your arms? No, I do not.

Adam didn't say this. Instead, he pretended to look for paperclips in the kitchen drawers. He pretended to look for them in his nearby backpack. He pretended for a solid minute.

"Guess I'm all out. Sorry."

Earlier that morning, Adam had stripped the house of paperclips, pencils, and any sharp objects he could find. He had left the knives in the kitchen drawer because their absence would invite too much suspicion. He just hoped Sutton wouldn't graduate from paperclip scratches to knife cuts.

Sutton sighed, pivoted like a military commander, and headed back to her bedroom. No goodnight, no birthday wish. Adam understood why people drank booze. Had he the taste for the stuff, he would have drowned out this moment as fast as humanly possible.

Turning out the lights in the hallway, Adam went to bed. He stared at the ceiling, hoping a solution would present itself. Irrespective of whether there was any merit to the Salem idea, Sutton would never accept it. She had rejected every offer Adam had made in the past three months.

Adam tossed and turned. He folded his pillow in half and removed the comforter. He then proceeded to put a second pillow under his head. Nothing worked. He stared at the alarm clock by his bedside, pleading with the dials to move faster. They didn't cooperate either.

Three hours later, Adam finally dozed off. If anyone were awake or taping this late-night event, they would have noticed a blue and gray cloud forming above Adam's sleeping body. It descended towards the one ear he had exposed. A voice, not specifically male or female, muttered, "*Let her.*"

Adam woke with a start. The voice chilled him to the bone. Disoriented, he needed to get his bearings. He checked the clock. It was 3:52 in the morning. He reached for his cell phone and dialed frantically. Terry answered on the first ring.

"Don't you ever sleep?" Adam asked.

"I'll sleep when it's coffin time," Terry bragged.

"You swear on your life that you heard the words—"

"*Let her*. And yes, I swear on everyone's life."

Adam wanted to avoid Salem. Almost more than that, he wanted to avoid his old partner, too. But he was desperate for a breakthrough with Sutton. His heart told him to barge into her room, drag her out of bed by the headphones, and take her to the local hospital for a mental check-up. So what if it cost him the relationship. She would get the proper medical treatment and, hopefully, live a full life.

On the other hand, his brain convinced him that a mental health facility wouldn't do the trick. Salem—the place he planned on never visiting again—was his only chance.

REGRESS

JONATHAN JENSEN COULD NOT BELIEVE his achievement. He officially hit the ten-year mark. No booze of any sort. Not even a sip. He headed outside his apartment for a moment and studied the October night. It was gray and windy. All he wanted was to celebrate.

He did not want to celebrate with seltzers.

He did not want to celebrate with sodas.

He did not want to celebrate with a foofoo coffee at the local café.

He did not want to celebrate with a box of pastries from his favorite bakery.

He wanted to celebrate by getting inebriated beyond belief.

Jonathan knew it would be an epic mistake. It wasn't wrong because it would end his decade-long streak sans alcohol; it was unwise because it would start a new decade of drinking.

He couldn't risk it. He had a quality girlfriend that didn't think alcohol was required to have a good time, and he had a teaching job at a hoity-toity prep school that, compared to others in surrounding areas, paid particularly well.

Jonathan refused to imbibe any alcohol that evening. However, Sally, the aforementioned partner, called to relay the fact that she wasn't coming home.

"Two nurses went home with the flu."

"That doesn't mean you have to stay for a double," Jonathan said.

"You know me. I can't say no."

The truth of the matter was that Sally often said no to the offerings of life. But she never turned down her boss. Jonathan didn't understand the hold that woman had over Sally, although if he had to venture a guess, it would have been akin to the power that booze had held over him in years past.

When Jonathan reflected upon his phone exchange with the one everybody said to "never let get away," he realized that she hadn't acknowledged the day's importance. He never kept his past and reasons for sobriety a secret. He had been candid with her about his issue from the jump.

Desperate to see if she was preoccupied or just didn't care,

Jonathan fired off a text that, if read correctly, would land like a guilt-filled missile.

"So much for celebrating tonight."

Sally saw the message instantly, but no reply came. Yes, she could become ultra busy in a matter of seconds. It shouldn't have mattered. At the very least, she could have replied right away with a frown emoji if she didn't have time to form the adequate words.

Jonathan stared at his phone. He disliked technological devices so much that he criticized those who were beholden to them. And yet, here he was, acting like the people he criticized. All he desired from Sally was a reply laced with recognition for his accomplishment and disappointment for her inability to join him in whatever booze-free activity he could find. A night of board games and take-out food would have sufficed!

Jonathan's impatience grew. He went over to the sink and studied the dishes filled to the brim. He hadn't left them there. Sally disliked emptying the dishwasher so much that she would leave all of her new dishes—the dirty ones—in the sink. On more than five occasions, Jonathan witnessed her opening the dishwasher to remove a clean bowl or spoon and then shutting the door. Under no circumstances would Sally do the dishes. He hated her for it. He hated her for not sending a text yet.

Jonathan emptied the dishwasher and cleaned out all of her disgusting dishes filled with oatmeal, soup, and cheese residue. He found a few strands of Sally's blond hair on the sink brush. Instead of freaking out, he calmly removed them. He would quickly retort the "never let her get away" argument with other behavioral ticks that few would be able to tolerate on a full-time basis.

Jonathan switched the vibrate setting to the ringer. In the mean-time, he occupied his brain with various tasks around the apartment. Task one: remove mold from the bathroom. He recently purchased a spray that one hundred percent guaranteed to eliminate mold within minutes.

Jonathan entered the bathroom and stared at the ceiling. In the middle of fading tan paint was an island of black mold that looked like an elementary art student's disastrous attempt to sketch out Florida.

Eleven minutes later, Jonathan had finished that task. He proceeded to the next one, which was ridding the refrigerator of any unused or expired food. When he opened the door, he found at least seven items—none belonging to him, by the way—that begged to be put out of their misery. There was a bag of mixed greens that weren't green anymore, a leftover piece of well-done steak that was forming white on its edges, an open package of sharp cheddar cheese that was not protected by a Ziploc bag, a white container of brown rice that—if memory served Jonathan correctly —was purchased at the Chinese restaurant two weeks ago, a bottle of sparkling cider without a cap on, an unopened container of guacamole that had become dark brown, and, last but not least, a container of tightly capped Simply orange juice without any more liquid inside.

Never let her get away? Jonathan thought. He wanted to offer her up to the highest bidder.

Jonathan received a reply from Sally sixty-two minutes after he texted her. The response?

"Why would we celebrate?"

This was the straw that broke the camel, or in this instance, Jonathan's back. He stared at the whiteboard in the corner of the living room. Written in blue letters, it said YEARS CLEAN with DAYS CLEAN right next to it. Sally knew he was about to cross this mark. He didn't know if her work commitments made her forget or if she genuinely didn't care about him meeting this goal. At least on three separate occasions, Jonathan recalled her asking if they could put the whiteboard elsewhere.

Occasion 1: "Does that have to be in the living room?"

Occasion 2: Can we take it down when guests come over?"

Occasion 3: Why do you have to broadcast the number?

Said three occasions happened during petty arguments that morphed into major ones. Jonathan stuck to his guns regarding the whiteboard because he liked the notion of owning his past. He found humility appealing in others. If the whiteboard made her uncomfortable, she had something brewing internally that needed to be confronted.

Jonathan stared at the text again. "Why would we celebrate?"

He considered a scathing reply. He did one better, however. He turned off his phone. Sally hated radio silence.

Jonathan removed the whiteboard from the wall, walked over to the open window, and dropped it four flights into a dumpster that had both flaps open as if to say, "I welcome all trash."

Less than an hour later, Jonathan found himself inside North Shore Beer Works. He scanned the place. There were only a handful of patrons. This didn't bother him. He kicked the night off with a beer. He would consume more potent liquids later.

Perked up by Halloween approaching in seven days, Jonathan ordered a pumpkin beer. He had never tried one before. He didn't know when the craft beer scene took off. The only thing he knew was that it exploded during his period of sobriety.

Jonathan thought the brown sugar on the rim was a bit over-the-top. When asked by the pregnant bartender whether he liked it or not, he told her it was "wonderful." Drinking anything was.

Despite being familiar with Salem after becoming a resident four years ago, Jonathan carried around a "Things To Do in Salem" map. He developed the following plan: he would wet his whistle at North Shore Beer Works. After knocking back a seasonal beer or two, he would venture on over to the Essex Tavern. While there, he would remain with beer since he whole-heartedly believed in the adage of "beer before liquor, never been sicker." Jonathan would conclude the night of debauchery with a visit to the Bell and Candle Distillery. He was more intrigued by their curated cocktails than a plastic liter of cheap spirit from the local package store. He had never treated himself in the past. Now he had the attitude and financial resources to do so.

As Jonathan neared the bottom of his glass, he experienced a prolonged moment of guilt. *Why did he do this? Why tonight?* He didn't lose a pet or loved one. An event like that warranted a mental slippage. Was this simply because his girlfriend, the one that everybody loved, didn't want to celebrate with him?

No, it wasn't about Sally's lack of celebration. It was her lack of appreciation for his noteworthy achievement. This, and only this, had forced Jonathan down a black hole.

"You okay, sweetie?" the bartender asked.

"Yeah, yeah, yeah. Just...thinking."

"Think less. Drink more."

Jonathan hesitated. He didn't know what he should say. The bartender slid a refill in front of him.

"On me."

The floodgates opened. Once he accepted the second beer, Jonathan knew that it would lead to a number most people would frown upon. He hoped that his tolerance for booze would be significantly less than it used to be. This way, he could have a few here and there, go home, and crawl into bed. Sally wouldn't be the wiser; the hospital scheduled her until five in the morning.

Jonathan accepted the second beer and made a note of when he received it. The first beer had taken thirty-four minutes to complete. He thought the new one would take much longer. He thought that would be the pattern for the rest of the night.

Jonathan finished beer number two in seventeen minutes. He compared his watch with the time of the receipt. Something had to be wrong.

"What time you have?" Jonathan asked the bartender.

Jonathan frowned when she informed him of the exact same time. He had consumed his second drink in half the time of the first one. He felt his old self screaming and begging for more.

Jonathan left a hefty tip on the bar and rushed out of the establishment. He thought the fresh air would make him feel better. If nothing else, it could help counter his nervous energy. But what was there to be anxious about? Didn't he want this?

His old self shouted, "Yes, yes, yes!" His new, boring self countered with "No, no, no."

Jonathan reflected on his history with alcohol. The amount he once consumed regularly never scared him since he didn't give one iota of thought to his health. What terrified him the most was the impact it had on his closest relationships.

His older brother, Peter, stopped talking to him fourteen years ago. Jonathan ruined the relationship by getting sloshed with vodka at his wife's baby shower. The event was hazy for two reasons: Jonathan didn't remember what he had done, and most of the witnesses refused to divulge what occurred. He apologized profusely, but the common reply to his gesture was "an apology isn't good enough." If an apology wasn't good enough, then what the heck was?

His younger sister Amanda stopped talking to him twelve years ago. Jonathan ruined the relationship during a housesitting stint. While she and her husband visited college friends in Tucson, Jonathan consumed every bottle in their liquor cabinet. His only responsibilities that week were to feed the fish, vacuum any room he stepped inside, and take out the trash and recycles. When Amanda and her husband arrived, they noticed that he hadn't done any of these tasks. As they counted the number of empty bottles, a burly African American policeman entered the home.

"So, a robber came into this home, and all they stole was…"

"The booze," Jonathan quickly stated.

The cop eyed Amanda. No one bought Jonathan's excuse. Similar to the incident with his brother, he apologized. The only issue with this apology was that it happened a year later via text. He never got a response.

His mother, the one in major denial about her youngest son's addiction, stopped talking to him ten and a half years ago. What began as a sweet dinner between mother and son turned sour when the topic of a teacher vacancy at her school came up.

"Get me an interview?"

Despite saying it like a question, Jonathan thought he was entitled to a chance because of his connection to her. *This was a world of nepotism after all*, he thought. But she rejected him; she had never done this before.

"It has taken me years to work up the courage to say this, but you have a problem. I will not recommend you for a job that puts you around impressionable children until you seek help."

Jonathan guzzled his red wine, shoved a turkey cutlet into his mouth, cussed at her, and left in a huff. One week later, he was in rehab.

Fast forward more than ten years ahead. He paced outside of North Shore Beer Works confused about which direction he wanted the night to go.

Booze was a relationship killer, he thought. If there were a bridge left to be burned, the alcoholic within him would indeed find it.

Jonathan headed in the direction of his apartment, surprisingly ready for this night to end. He didn't trust himself. He needed to get home before he made a decision he would later regret.

Neither Sally nor his job were perfect in any way, but both provided him with sanity and stability that allowed him to survive.

Jonathan turned off Derby Street and made it to Liberty Street. His apartment complex was less than a hundred yards away. His best self was about to get the victory.

SALLY CHECKED HER PHONE. No response from Jonathan. It was the longest gap in communication since they began dating thirteen months ago. She rationalized it easily. She committed to a double; he knew enough not to bother her. But she sent him three check-in texts! What did they amount to? Not a single reply. None of them, according to her phone, were even seen. As much as she convinced herself not to worry, she was a tad concerned.

Sally made her way down the hallway to the electronic punch-out clock (yes, her hospital still had one), typed in her key code, and ventured towards the elevator.

This double shift kicked her ass. Regardless, she was the one who decided to stay. She could have turned down her boss. *Why couldn't she turn down her boss?*

Inside the elevator, Sally received a text from a co-worker. It said, "Emergency. Go to Bay Ridge immediately." She didn't work in Bay Ridge. She had no clue why a co-worker would summon her to the mental health and substance abuse treatment area.

"I just did a double," she typed back.

"Trust me. Get here ASAP."

Sally fought back what felt like a million yawns and pivoted in the direction of Bay Ridge. She had no idea what to expect. She spent all of her time in Addison Gilbert. She had zero experience in Bay Ridge. Why, after a double, did she have to go to that location?

Twelve minutes later, Sally had her answer. The co-worker directed Sally to a room at the end of the hall. The room had one patient: her boyfriend, Jonathan. Sally covered her mouth in horror as a nurse pumped his stomach. Her eyes drifted towards an abandoned white polo on a vacant chair. It was Jonathan's shirt; she purchased it for him at Gap a month ago. She picked it up. Written in black Sharpie was one question: *Why didn't you celebrate with me?*

STORAGE FACILITY

JACKIE INTENDED to be at the storage facility for less than five minutes. Her plan was simple: she would park her blue Chevy Silverado, hop out with a fourteen ounce can of Raid, and blast all of the contents onto an unruly hornets' nest that hung approximately three feet above her husband's Brinks Commercial Disco Lock.

Like all plans, this one took an unforeseen detour. The surprise, however, was not related to the reason she was there. The operation appeared to be a resounding success. Foam expanded around the nest; a handful of hornets flew out. The rest would be dead in minutes.

Jackie returned to her truck and put her seat belt on. Before she grabbed the door handle, she heard it. A whimper.

A country tune played on the radio. Jackie focused intently on the song's lyrics. A thirty-something country boy crooned about his drunk adventures with buddies the night his high school sweetheart served him divorce papers. She turned off the radio.

Save a few chirping crickets, the evening scene was silent. Jackie could leave knowing that whatever she had heard was over or unreal —the result of her overworked mind playing tricks on her. She had completed three double shifts for her bus company this week. She didn't mind; she had to push herself to the limit after fighting through a global pandemic that, according to experts, rivaled the Great Depression. Her husband, eighteen years her senior, wasn't helping much with finances after his department strongly encouraged him to take early retirement.

Unlike her husband, Jackie was a fighter that never would have accepted a modified deal that jeopardized her future. Her husband was a passive man. Despite being what most would call a "satisfactory woodshop teacher," he led a sedentary existence that only intensified when his superiors ordered him to head off into the proverbial sunset.

Jackie listened for new sounds. A bullfrog made his appearance known. It was evident by his tone that he desired a companion for the evening. She laughed. But her amusement ended when she heard another whimper. While the previous one had been short and isolated, this one continued for what felt like a full minute.

Jackie opened her glove box, removed a flashlight passed down through generations from her hardware store owning Great Grandpa, and twisted the top until the light came on.

Jackie looked behind her. She shined the flashlight at all the doors of the units. None were open. She turned her attention to the six units, three on each side, that were ahead of her. She aimed her light along the left side. All of those doors were closed. She aimed her light along the right side.

The last door was wide open.

Jackie's stomach grumbled. She knew it wasn't because she hadn't eaten anything. She had wolfed down a footlong tuna fish sandwich from Subway less than ninety minutes ago. No, her stomach told her that checking out what was inside that last door would be a mistake of epic proportions.

Regardless of her stomach's warnings, Jackie pressed on with cautious steps. While her brain formulated all of the disturbing possibilities that might lie within the unit, her heart convinced her that she needed to pursue the truth at all costs if it meant saving an injured child.

Jackie closed her eyes for a moment, took a breath, and entered the unit. She paused immediately. The space appeared empty. It wasn't until she stepped in a bit farther that she noticed a table with a black device sitting atop it.

Jackie rubbed her eyes to make sure she wasn't hallucinating. She approached the table and held her light above the black object. It was an old Casio tape player. She laughed at the absurdity of one of these being saved. It must have been thirty years old.

Jackie relaxed once she knew there was no whimpering girl. There was only the tape of a girl whimpering. She hit *stop* on the player and ejected the tape. But then it dawned on her how creepy the situation was and she quickly turned to leave.

A male figure stood tall outside the unit. Jackie couldn't make out his age or ethnicity. All she noticed were black glasses and black clothing. Before she communicated with him, the door to the unit slammed shut.

Panic eluded Jackie for a moment, believing this was all some twisted prank. But her husband had a dry—not dark—sense of humor, and he didn't have any friends. Panic arrived once she heard the door lock.

Over the next forty-eight hours, the local cops and detectives studied the scene of the crime. Time was precious. The longer a missing-person case went, the likelihood of the victim being saved, or found alive, was diminished.

Two problems prevented the authorities from piecing together what happened to Jackie Fuller of Danvers, Massachusetts. Problem one was this: storage unit C-1 was spotless. The table and recorder (objects they weren't aware of) were gone. There wasn't a hair, fingerprint, or speck of saliva anywhere. The only elements available to guide their efforts were Jackie's abandoned Chevy Silverado and a camera from the neighboring D units. The camera pointed right at the front of the unit that Jackie entered. This is the camera that told them to search the unit. Despite the footage being grainy, the cops watched their subject, Jackie, as she vacated her running vehicle to approach whatever was inside the space. The video feed stopped right at that specific moment. This was problem number two.

Days passed. Then weeks. Jackie's husband became restless. He called the Salem Police Department on an hourly basis. The cops grew tired of his vitriolic tone and irrational theories. He sensed their frustration. However, he rationalized why they should take all of his words seriously. He was a citizen of the United States of America. He was Jackie's loving husband. He was a fan of those crime shows on the ID network, which, in his eyes, elevated him to an equal footing with the local authorities.

After three months, the cops gave up. Jackie's husband surrendered, as well. None of his theories panned out. To make matters worse, he developed prostate cancer. His doctor informed him that his life would have been longer if he believed in preventative measures. Jackie's husband didn't. He had less than six months to live.

If he were a detective and had his druthers, he would have checked every single unit at the storage facility. He never explained to the cops why this impulse arrived; the idea came in a nightmare.

The manager of the facility never checked all of the units. The cops and detectives didn't either. Had they done so, they would have discovered the bound and gagged lifeless body of Jackie Fuller in a unit adjacent to the one where she had found the whimpering tape player.

MISTER SHOTGUN

WHENEVER MIKEY ENTERED a room with his father present, the result was the same. The man stood up from his rocking chair, snarled, cocked his double-barrel shotgun, and aimed it at his only child.

Mikey's go-to response of "Dad, it's me" never worked.

His father, diagnosed with early Alzheimer's a month back, had gone from a fully functional being with gainful employment at the local lumber yard to a certifiable nutcase who was afraid to leave his home. His boss at the lumberyard contacted Mikey at school.

Mikey was doodling on his notebook during Anatomy and Physiology class when the phone rang. The teacher, a sub that day, informed Mikey that he was due in the Main Office for an emergency. He disliked that the substitute announced this fact to the group; he hated having the spotlight on himself.

When he got to the Main Office, his father's boss, Mr. Richardson, was waiting in a comfy chair. Mikey assumed his father was dead or in the hospital. He was wrong about both.

"Mikey, I, uh, talk to you outside for a minute?"

"Is my dad okay?"

"Outside, please."

Mr. Richardson whipped out his cell phone, cued up a video, and pressed play.

"I didn't tape it to make fun. I taped it so you can get the whole picture."

There was nothing special about the video. His father unloaded lumber for a pair of customers, what appeared to be a married couple. Mikey turned to Richardson to convey his disappointment.

"Be patient," Richardson advised.

Mikey glued his eyes to the phone screen. That is when he saw it. His father snapped. He swung the lumber at the husband's head. Luckily, the man ducked in time, or else he would have spent the evening in the hospital or worse. The wife ran off camera. Multiple employees approached Mikey's father. He tried to strike them as well. They knocked the lumber out of his hands, pinned him down, and tied him up.

"He's at the walk-in, getting his brain checked out," Richardson shared.

"Why couldn't I hear the audio?"

"Don't blame me. Blame the feed from my store cameras."

"What was he saying?"

Mikey retrieved his father at the walk-in. The doctor informed Mikey that his father had an episode. Mikey processed this much better than what the boss told him, that his father was worried zombies were going to attack.

Mikey didn't have a mother to lean on. No brothers or sisters. No connection with a teacher at school. The only person he called was his father's sister, Tammy. She lived in a trailer park in Arkansas, monumentally far—in distance and lifestyle—from his community of Salem.

Mikey had met her twice in all his sixteen years. Both times she wasn't cordial. He expected no different this time around. Moments after Mikey told her about his father's/her brother's diagnosis, she chuckled.

"I knew he'd get that. Our daddy had that. His daddy did as well. The men in this family go cuckoo. You're next, kiddo."

No concern. No offers of verbal, physical, or monetary assistance. No indication of love anywhere. Mikey was screwed.

Mikey took a few days off from school to address his father's new condition. He read everything he could about Alzheimer's disease; he believed he could take care of his father if he educated his brain on the pros, cons, and intricacies of the subject.

Night one, two, three and four ended with Mikey's father and the shotgun. While it bothered Mikey to have a lethal gun aimed at his chest (Monday), his neck (Tuesday), his temple (Wednesday), and his mouth (Thursday), he believed that he, via love and understanding, could make his father better.

Mikey knew that the "Dad, it's me" approach had to be abandoned and fast. It triggered something within his father that took several minutes to resolve. But what could Mikey do? What would help his father's condition? The recently prescribed pills had not solved the problem; as a matter of fact, they seemed to only exacerbate matters.

Mikey had a sleepless night while developing plans to save his father. It wasn't until 4:18 in the morning when he stumbled upon an idea that gave him hope. He stepped out of his bedroom, took a few steps down the hallway, and peeked on his father's status.

His father, snoring heavily, rocked back and forth in a rocking chair that he stole from the local dump. Mikey knew the time was now.

He cleared his throat and altered his posture. He messed up his hair next and started drooling. If his father's whole mental world relied on zombies attacking, then Mikey would commit to that acting job like Al Freaking Pacino.

Mikey groaned upon his entrance to the room. His father's epic snores stopped on a dime. Mikey increased his volume. His father's eyes popped open. It was here when Mikey saw it—a flash of sheer joy across his father's eyes. He saw his old father in this moment. The quiet but loving man who catered to his son's every need. This tender scene lasted less than five seconds because his father sprung from the rocking chair wielding the double-barrel.

"Leave my family alone, or so help me God!"

The fact that his father mentioned family made Mikey's zombie transformation all the more meaningful. His father cocked the shotgun and aimed it. Despite the discomfort of having a lethal weapon aimed at his heart, Mikey relaxed knowing that he had removed the bullets from the chamber on Tuesday night. This moment, like the others, would pass. His father would plop back into the chair; Mikey would return to bed. But that didn't happen.

The blast sent Mikey sailing through the air; he felt like he was up there for minutes on end. During his sudden trajectory, he wondered when and why his father had reloaded the chamber. More importantly, he wondered if his father had bouts of sanity that he wasn't aware of since this whole thing started.

When Mikey landed on the floor, he inspected his wound. His

insides were oozing out of his frail body. He knew little of human expiration, but he assumed he had less than two minutes left.

"Got you, you son of a bitch ass zombie."

Mikey's father smiled and then leaned the shotgun next to his rocking chair. Mikey watched this play out. He had never seen his father so content. And while Mikey would miss his father and some aspects of life (manga, energy drinks, a snow day), he relished the fact that he would never get the chance to lose his mind. That type of exit from the world was frightening, way more frightening than a shotgun blast.

SAMSARA

THE SIMPLE AND universally understood feeling of needing that first drink of the day is what altered Babs' fate.

She learned of a new brewery—at least new to her—in the Salem area called Ghouls Amok Beer Company. Even though she was partial to wine, she was tiring of the offerings. A red wine made her yawn quickly, and white wine kept her up most of the night since it rarely had any impact on her.

Beer was different. The range of flavors from an IPA to a Saison to a Sour to a Pilsner to a Stout was unlike anything she had ever encountered in wine.

Since Babs became a day drinker—she wouldn't admit this to anyone except herself—she looked for new and exciting ways to stimulate her day. She drove anywhere in her birth state so long as the venue was new. While this hinted at an adventurous spirit, Babs knew it had more to do with not being in the same place twice. She was on the run from herself, and no one but her knew it.

As she eluded torrential rain that the weather girl had failed to include in the morning forecast, Babs reached the door handle of Ghouls Amok. She tugged. Locked. She checked her watch: 11:39. She studied their sign. They opened at noon. She had twenty-one minutes to kill.

She paced back and forth outside the door. She instantly realized that this was a bad look, especially since no one else was doing it with her.

She scanned her surroundings. There weren't many options. But as luck would have it, a craft and curated goods shop was right next door. She glanced at signs in the window that advertised classes for taxidermy and magical mediation. She didn't care one bit about the latter. But the former intrigued her.

Babs poked around Wind & Wax and tried to process its eccentric interior. She bumped into a display case. A ginger-haired clerk with indecipherable age told her to watch her step. Babs wanted to exit the store in a huff. Unfortunately for her, she had eighteen more minutes to kill before a beertender could supply her with a fresh pint.

The clock couldn't tick fast enough. Time pissed Babs right off. It slowed when you wanted it to speed up and vice versa. She picked up overpriced books. She bent down to glance at the artwork that wouldn't sell anywhere but here. She fixed the Persian rug that had caused her to stumble. All of these actions only took four minutes. That meant fourteen more minutes to go. And she had already done one lap around the entire interior!

This wasn't true. Babs somehow overlooked the taxidermy section. She fixed her eyes on a light brown bat that must have perished mid-yawn or mid-scream. It had black markings on its fully spread out wings. It looked like it wanted to pounce on whoever stood in front of it. Babs left Mr. Bat alone.

Babs studied a few of the other stuffed victims that graced the walls. There was the head of a whitetail deer whose eyes suggested that he had harbored different plans than this for his future; there was an Alaskan moose head that appeared to have left this world with a smirk; and, finally, there was a red fox, positioned like a Playboy centerfold, perched up by its very own tree stump.

Babs didn't have good credit or much in the name of savings. Otherwise, she would have walked with the three heads. The thought made her chuckle. She liked the image of driving across American Legion Highway with three animal heads as her front and back seat passengers.

Babs headed towards the exit and read the names of various candles. She rechecked the watch. Nine minutes to go! Time was her fiercest enemy.

She lifted a candle labeled "Bark Nights" and absentmindedly lowered it into her pocket. The ginger-haired clerk caught her in the act. Babs didn't try to explain; she simply put the candle back on its display. While she was certainly game for a fight, it could result in her getting kicked out of the store. The risk of employees from Ghouls Amok witnessing such an encounter would embarrass her and convince her to go elsewhere. But she didn't want to go elsewhere. She wanted a beer.

With no rhyme or reason, the hair on Babs' arms rose. She couldn't remember the last time she had goosebumps. She thought it was at her husband's wake eleven months ago. Right as visitors walked in to pay their respects, the lights flickered and then went out. Most people thought it was an electrical issue. Some believed that it was the by-product of an earlier storm. A select few blamed it on the twisted humor of Babs' husband. Oh, how they chuckled at this possibility.

Babs found it humorless. For one, she believed in spirits. And two, she thought her husband would torment her if given a chance. She had treated him like dirt throughout their twenty-one-year marriage. She put her needs first. She never listened to him. She barely cooked. She never complimented him. She avoided all forms of intimacy with him. She bullied him into believing that she was worth having. The truth of the matter was she had no clue why he suffered through her frequent crap. During a heated argument one night, Babs challenged him with the "Why do you put up with me?" question. Her husband's response was quick and concise: "Cuz' I believe what goes around, comes around..."

Was this her husband's doing? Why was she having a visceral reaction to nothing in particular?

She glanced in the direction of the taxidermy bat again; it stared right back at her. Babs swore that its eyes moved. Perhaps a patron had lifted it to check the price. However, her dark mind had other ideas.

Babs walked towards an oak table. She pressed her right index finger against a box of tarot cards and pulled it back; dust now covered her finger. Someone, or everyone, was getting paid a whole lot to do nothing around here.

Babs turned quickly and made eyes with the bat. His eyes were closed. She covered her mouth in shock. She prayed that sudden vision loss was the culprit and that she would rectify the situation later after a pit stop at America's Best. Her vision was twenty-twenty. Her prayers were not likely to be answered.

She removed her watch from her pocket. She couldn't wait to get the hell out of this place. Only two minutes left! She regained her composure. Two minutes was an absolute breeze.

She couldn't get the bat out of her mind. She spun around and grabbed the nearest item for sale: a pair of wooden Day of the Dead earrings. Eighteen dollars was a fair price.

"All earrings are ten percent off. I'm finishing the sign now," the clerk announced.

Babs never purchased items this strange, but she decided to go for it to appease the pushy clerk and to shift her attention away from the ominous bat. All she had to do in the next sixty seconds was buy the damn earrings, leave, and walk next door. That is how close she was to getting her first beer of the day.

The clerk scanned the package. The total appeared on the screen.

"Thirty-six dollars?! I thought those were eighteen."

"Eighteen instead of thirty-six?" the clerk asked rudely.

Babs and the clerk engaged in a staring contest. Even Babs could delay the consumption of a beer to assure the victory. The clerk removed the earrings from the bag and walked towards the jewelry table. This tiny moment caused Babs to look at the bat a final time.

It winked at her. Babs screamed.

Overwhelmed by what she knew had to be the taunts of her deceased husband, Babs backed out of the store, shaking her head. She was delirious. The clerk's jaw dropped. The handful of other patrons watched in wide-eyed horror as Babs made her way into the middle of the street. The second the clerk tried to inform Babs about the earrings' correct price, a black Chevy Traverse rammed into Babs' kneecaps and sent her flying into the air.

The clerk rushed to the register station to call 911. A patron whipped out their cell phone and recorded the scene on the street.

Babs lifted her bloody face off the pavement and noticed that the front door to Ghouls Amok was opening. A curvy blonde kicked a doorstop three times before it held the door back. The blonde went pale when she noticed Babs.

Babs held her hand out and pleaded. "It was him. I swear to you. The. Bat. Was. Him."

SUTTON FROST

HER FATHER WASN'T the only one surprised by her acceptance of a Salem trip; she, too, was unprepared for her immediate "Yes." But getting away from school for a few days after requesting to follow your crush, dropping a complimentary note to said crush, and receiving no response, made Sutton beyond amenable to leaving not only the state but her home country.

Sutton zipped her duffle bag halfway and then stopped. She had packed up too fast. It hadn't provided the distraction she wanted. She unzipped the bag, flipped it over, and let the clothes fall out. She started folding clothes again, hoping that it would take her mind off Zoe Wilde. She wondered: *If this is what having a crush felt like, why did people choose to like anybody?*

Sutton opened Insta and rechecked her feed. No messages. No likes. Her short life amounted to little more than posts of random musicians she discovered on Spotify and images from the graphic novel she was attempting to write. No one cared about the musicians she recommended; no one cared about her artwork except for two people: her sad sack of a father and his former business partner Terry Dennis. Besides them, she had nine others following her. Not exactly a positive when you aim to make friends.

Sutton clicked on the search icon and typed in Zoe Wilde for the seventh day in a row. She perked up at the sight of a new pic. It displayed Zoe tugging on her new purple locks and sticking her tongue out. The caption read, "Boo!"

Sutton moved her finger to the heart button. But she froze. It would appear desperate. She'd sent a note three hours ago, praising Zoe for her boots (black Doc Marten's). How pathetic would it be to like this new pic and send another note? It would be uber-pathetic. Sutton powered off her cell, actually complying with her dad's "Phone off by ten" rule.

She ignored the pile of clothes in front of her and whipped out the composition notebook that contained her graphic novel's workings. It was called *The Fun Ends in Connecticut,* and it revolved around a girl who befriended demons at the local cemetery to cure her constant boredom in the worst state in America.

She sketched a picture of a middle-aged woman pushing a baby stroller past a graveyard. Trepidation was on the woman's face, but the lead girl in the story waved her towards the entrance gate. A bubble quote revealed the girl's words: "It's safe. Trust me, I'm no liar." Five headstones down the graveled pathway hid the ugliest demons an aspiring artist could generate.

Sutton sighed and closed her notebook. She powered on the phone. She checked Insta once more. The status quo remained. No response from Zoe. The fact that her crush posted two new stories informed Sutton that she had seen the follow request and the message. Zoe ignored them because she didn't like Sutton at all. The devil was definitely in those details.

Sutton tossed the phone aside. She scanned the room for something sharp. Under the oak dresser, she spotted what she couldn't find earlier in the night: a paperclip.

THE AGED MAN

BERNIE ALWAYS WANTED to be a Bernadette. He didn't think this dream —which he kept secret from his family and wife of thirty-eight years —would ever be fully realized. A part of this was undoubtedly his lack of confidence; the other part related to the fact that he was approaching the ripe old age of ninety. His family was long gone, and his wife, trooper from the start, passed away one week ago while attempting to carve a pumpkin.

Today was the day for Bernie to become a woman.

He inched his way down the winding staircase from the third-floor unit. He paused along the way to regain his breath and composure. The idea of being exposed for what he was terrified him. Regardless, he, after years of being a prisoner to his mind, officially felt like his true self.

Once he stepped onto the sidewalk, he avoided a dreadlocked skateboarder. The kid, quick on his feet, yelled, "Watch it, lady!"

While Bernie didn't particularly care to be screamed at in public, he took solace in the fact that the kid referred to him as a woman. This was a promising start to the day!

The sole mission for his day was to have the gall to leave the unit in women's garb, and to, eventually, invade the community of those at the Home For Aged Gentlewomen. He thought visiting other locations in the city would open the door for both criticism and skepticism. The ladies at the Home for Aged Gentlewomen were either ten years his junior or none his senior. If he could blend in there, he would develop the confidence to blend in at other locations.

His plan, or excuse, was to gain entrance into the home and pretend to be a relative of one of the residents. The likelihood of finding a woman to dupe was on his side because they all, at least according to a recent retiree, were suffering from a mental or physical condition. Bernie aimed to find a lady that was struggling with the former.

Bernie glanced at the Salem Harbor and then entered through the cast-iron gate. He perked up internally; he'd never thought he would make it this far. Certainly, someone would have outed him by now.

He marveled at the brick exterior of the building. He couldn't believe that such an old building could look so new.

He made his way up a set of stairs, removed a batch of sunflowers from the pair of black pots, and knocked on the black door.

No one answered. Perhaps this was the norm. He tried the handle. Miraculously, it opened!

He stepped into the home, expecting a guard or employee with some degree of authority to stop him. This did not happen.

He heard a commotion coming from a room in the distance. He walked ahead, feeling more like a spy than a man dressed in women's garb. He passed three vacant rooms before arriving at one that had bodies present.

A game of bingo was in session. But this was no typical game. The announcer, a busty brunette sporting a Tufts tee with track jacket wrapped around her waist, repeated the number and letter combinations ad nauseam. Said announcer took notice of Bernie. He froze in the hallway, assuming that the jig was officially up.

"Did you want to join us?" the brunette asked.

Bernie considered mimicking a woman's voice. But he quickly recalled how many people in his lifetime said that he had a deep voice. For this reason, he relied on the fail-safe head nod.

The brunette waved him in. Seven ladies, some with and without their marbles, stared at him with disdain. He parked a seat in a chair that looked like it hailed from Victorian times.

The brunette handed him a game board and the necessary materials. She announced the start of a new game. And Bernie, pretending to be Bernadette, was on cloud nine. He had pulled it off. Not only had he convinced a skater, but he was able to convince an entire room (with questionable faculties for sure) that he was, in fact, a she.

Bingo started like it always did. However, had Bernie read the room, he would have noticed that a woman who looked older than dirt was studying his every move. The brunette called B-13, then G-32. The group of ladies, including Bernie in disguise, played without offering a word or response. A few minutes passed. No one seemed to be gaining a lead in the game. Everything was peaceful until the brunette called O-64.

Bernie, hyper-aware of his untested voice, raised his right arm. The brunette studied him.

"You have a question?"

Bernie scanned the room for a writing utensil. None in sight. He cleared his throat. Then, he muttered the following:

"I have Bingo."

Now, had Bernie read the room, he would have noticed the death glares coming his way from the woman who looked as if she had stepped out of a coffin only moments earlier. But he didn't read the room. He basked in the glory of belonging to his desired group.

A lot happened in this particular moment, however. The brunette tried to review Bernie's board to see if he was the winner. An Italian woman with a yellow cat t-shirt congratulated Bernie. And the death glare woman, with all her displayed hate, somehow managed to be overlooked by everyone. This provided her with the opportunity she had been dreaming of since Bernie, woman or not, had entered the musty room.

As the brunette approached Bernie to check out his board, the death glare woman lunged towards him with the rage of a wild animal. She whipped out a penknife (that no one knew she possessed) and plunged it straight into his heart. The brunette wailed. The aged women watched in a state of paralysis. Some knew what was happening while others appeared oblivious to this newfound horror show.

The death glare woman removed the penknife and hammered it into a new location on Bernie's body. She did all this, repeatedly, without interruption. The only words that left her lips were these:

"You are not the winner."

The brunette ran out of the room, claiming that she was going to call 911. The aged women did nothing but stare and whisper. The death glare woman stood in front of the group and smiled. Out of breath, she raised the penknife to her mouth and licked it.

"No one beats me at Bingo. No one!"

Bernie received the vicious pen attacks without batting an eye. He certainly didn't like being stabbed to death. But he counted his losses in life and thought that this moment—albeit painful and traumatizing —was more comfortable to take than confessing his womanly desires to his doting wife or ultra-conservative parents. This was the reason that he, after each puncture, maintained a smile on his face.

Bernie had made it through the morning as a woman. While the dream was exceptionally short, he had achieved it. The fact that he would be dead in a few minutes was utterly irrelevant.

FREEWRITE FRIDAY

IN HER THIRTY-SEVEN years of teaching, Barbara Fredericks had never joined her students in Freewrite Friday. Today was different, though. It was, after all, her final day of working in education, and she figured, for no other reason than to amuse herself, she would go out with a literal bang.

Said bang wasn't apparent to any of her students; for all they knew, she was simply killing time—like them—before a few select students would be selected to share their work of fiction or non.

Barb had already selected the students beforehand even though she would go through the laborious motions of pulling tickets from an old mason jar. Her chosen ones consisted of William Radcliffe, G.G. Hunt, and Elijah Woods. William made the cut because he was the best writer in the bunch. He was her only student who understood the difference between commas and semicolons. Beyond his aptitude for grammar, he would generate works of fiction that kept an audience hanging onto their seats. He knew that keeping an audience engaged was essential if you had any hope as a writer.

G.G. Hunt was second on the list for one reason only: she was on the autism spectrum. While she had a flair for creating exciting scenarios, she would, during a read aloud, veer off course and start improvising what was to come next. This drove all of her peers batty; it made Barbara adore her even more.

Elijah Woods was last on Barbara's list even though, in her mind, he was the only one she wanted to listen to every week. Elijah didn't know the difference between commas and semicolons. He didn't become upset with his work and edit it as he read. Oh no. He always read his work in the manner in which it was written: with total conviction.

Furthermore, his work was a continuation of the same story. The primary conflict revolved around a man with a drinking problem. Perhaps because he knew that his audience was between ten and eleven years old, Elijah made his main character addicted to energy drinks instead of alcohol. Or maybe he was speaking to his teacher via the character's plight to inform her that his father had a problem with booze and that he was a nightly danger to his mother, brother, and three older sisters.

On a typical Freewrite Friday, Barbara would transition to snack time once the students finished sharing their work. Not today, however. She would hop on the red stool in the front of the room and share her piece. Aside from modeling the ins and outs of grammar, sentence starters, and strategies for introductions and conclusions, Barbara had never shared an ounce of her work.

Today she would alter the status quo; today, she would blow their minds.

As promised, William went first. The others slated to share had no problem with the assigned order. There was no telling week-to-week what William would write about; the one aspect that could be guaranteed was that it would be flawless in the grammar department.

William was less than thirty seconds into his piece when Barbara realized what he was about to accomplish. She prided herself on her teaching abilities, but this idea of his was noteworthy and somewhat altruistic.

Students had been struggling with comma placement all year. This forced Barbara to revisit the area and concoct more engaging lessons than the previous one. Sometimes she was successful; other times, she was not.

For William, the gifted student who had been shipped from this school to that one by his helicopter mother, it was a frustrating thing to witness. Yes, Barbara provided him with plenty of tasks that nearly met his academic level. He was thankful for that. But the way the others struggled with something as simple as commas altered his view of education.

Regardless, he believed that he could be the one to inspire a group of eighteen classmates.

William's story was about a man name Comma and his cousin, the Semicolon. Students laughed at the absurdity of the information at the start of William's reading; however, they fell in line when they saw that he, and Mrs. Fredericks, meant business. Barbara marveled at how the story had everything: a protagonist you rooted for, a brilliant plot, snappy dialogue, and a conclusion that built up to a crescendo of humor. As if that were not enough, the students seemed to have learned the difference between commas and semicolons.

William asked, "Does everyone get it now?"

A majority of the students nodded or shouted out (risking a warning from their strict teacher) that they got it. A feeling of jealousy rushed through Barbara's mind. The feeling didn't last long as Barbara's eyes drifted to her "Teacher of the Year" plaque. Yes, it was from nine years ago. *But it still mattered*, she thought.

William sat in the back with a teacher's confidence and put his feet up on the desk. Barbara glared at him with such venom that his feet fell to the floor instantly. He yelled, "Ow!" as his heels smacked the floor.

"Do you need to visit the nurse?

"I'm good!"

G.G. waited in front of the room while this played out. Barbara walked to the sink area in the back of the room, pressed the power button on her blue Keurig, and turned to face the next speaker.

"What are we waiting for, G.G?"

"I was waiting for you."

"Begin."

G.G. shared a fictitious story about the second-to-last piece of bread in a bag that didn't want to be toasted. As the days of the week passed, various members of the Breadeater family removed pieces of bread from the bag for their morning toast.

One of the family members would toast the second-to-last piece of bread the next morning. He asked the last piece in the bag if he wanted to switch places.

"It wouldn't matter if we did. No one will toast me."

"No one?"

"That's what I've heard. I wish I had a solution for you, but I don't."

Staying true to form, G.G.'s story veered off course at the most exciting part. This was always disheartening for Barbara Fredericks. Although today, she wasn't the only audience member upset by the complete pivot towards something else. The students nearly revolted when G.G. rambled on to a nonfiction story about individual family members that eat toast, hate toast, and consider toast to be something only worthy of getting at a diner.

G.G.'s words went by unnoticed at this point, so much so that she ended up walking back to her seat in what could have, and certainly looked like shame.

Elijah Woods, sensitive as the day is long, made a pit stop to check on G.G.'s emotional state. Then, he ventured towards the front of the room, scanned the crowd, glanced at his notebook, and said the following:

"He didn't know it would be his last energy drink. The end."

The class erupted once Elijah said the word "end." For one, his story-shares were usually a page or two long. All he shared today was a single sentence before declaring that the story he had been working on since September was, like it or not, officially over.

Most were annoyed that he had wasted the class' time. A few students raised their hands, begging to share their stories. Barbara ignored them.

Because they thought share time was over, a few students made a break for the cubby areas to collect their snacks.

"Stay in your seats!"

"But it's snack time," Rees said with a challenging tone.

"Rees: It isn't snack time until I say it's snack time."

"What the h—"

"Don't finish that question unless you want to spend the rest of the day in the principal's office."

Rees refrained from continuing. Barbara walked to the back of the room and sat on a red stool that one of her former students had made for her in Woodworking 101. The students were hysterical; they got antsy when things deviated from the usual plan. Barbara eyed her crowd.

"Table 1 may join me on the purple mat."

Table 1 did so without complaint. Table 3 was next, followed by Table 2. Most of the students were beyond curious; they didn't dare act up. That said, Table 4 failed to receive an invite because Rees was at it again. Barbara didn't need to say anything to him. His table peers and classmates on the mat were ready to guide him to the principal's office themselves.

Rees still didn't get the message. His snack, and when he ate it, were of the utmost importance. Any change in that plan meant he would be texting his mother at lunch to complain about his harsh and irrational teacher.

"Everyone at Table 4 is invited to the mat except Rees."

"But...

"You sit in that seat or go to the principal's office. And complaining about me to your mother won't get you very far because it's my last day."

"Thank God," he said under his breath.

Typically, Barbara would elevate her intensity to the point where Rees would simply surrender. Not today, though. She wasn't going to let him railroad her attempt to share a personal story.

To make the wound sink in even deeper, Barbara resorted to a tactic that she might consider downright cruel if she weren't going to be a retired educator in a few short hours.

Betsy Bloom, a girl obsessed with unicorns and llamas, had recently become the object of Rees' affection. Barbara noticed that Betsy didn't reciprocate any of the attention he dished out. Based on months of observation, Barbara noticed that Betsy delivered all of her attention to female classmates and none of her male ones. Rees was too young and dumb to see this. One couldn't blame him. He was, after all, a fourth-grader. Regardless, Barbara used his crush against him to send the proverbial kill shot.

"Betsy, be a dear and go dial 112."

Proud to be of service, Betsy marched over to the phone.

"It's ringing."

"Great. After you're done, pick something from the prize box. There might be a new llama sticker in there."

Betsy's round eyes expanded with anticipation. The prospect of a new llama-related item made her ready to sell anyone down the river.

"They just answered."

"Tell them Mrs. Fredericks is sending Rees Fulton to the principal's office for disruptive behavior."

Rees went pink. Barbara struck a major nerve by making his crush the messenger. Tears trickled down his fat face.

"I'm…

"Are you *still* talking?"

Betsy gripped the phone with all her might and delivered this paraphrased message: "Mrs. Fredericks is sending Rees Fulton to the principal for, like, super bad behavior."

This sent Rees into a sobbing fit. As it continued for ten seconds, Barbara made a move towards him. He bolted from his chair, tripped over another at the neighboring table, and hurried out of the room.

Somewhat wrong or partially right, Barbara couldn't decide. It would be something for her to ponder on the deck later with a stiff gin and tonic within her grasp.

Barbara opened her composition notebook and began to read. There weren't any explanations necessary after the drama that occurred with Rees. Students gave her their undivided attention.

"This story is called *Smother*."

Barbara fell into a coughing fit. She reached around for her water bottle, but it was nowhere in sight. Still buzzing from the high of carrying out Rees' execution, Betsy ran over to Mrs. Frederick's table, snagged a bright pink Nalgene bottle, and delivered it back to her teacher with pride. Barbara guzzled it. Her coughing stopped. It wasn't without its cost, however. Water had trickled down all over her brand-new blouse.

"To all you wantrepreneurs out there, I beg you to create a water bottle that doesn't leak."

"Mine doesn't leak," Jessa Rhodes added. To sell her point, she tipped her Camelbak over. Water went everywhere. Students groaned at her foolish act.

"It's just water. Relax."

"I'm not sitting in a pool of w—"

Barbara slammed her composition book shut. Because Tommy

Slade didn't want to receive the same fate as Rees, he made a minor body adjustment to avoid the spill.

"Without further ado, I present my story. It might be fact. It might be fiction. You decide.."

Students shuffled their butts in place. They wouldn't miss this for the world. Mrs. Fredericks, an overly private teacher, never ponied up the goods on any personal question. This lack of vulnerability made her hard to read and even harder to please. Were a colleague or adult to confront Mrs. Fredericks about this fact later, she would claim that it was a tactic all teachers should utilize if they intended to have satisfactory learning paired with effective classroom management.

The story started rather dull. Barbara revealed nothing more than where this female teacher was raised (Hartford, Connecticut) and where she ended up (Salem, Massachusetts) after marrying at the ripe age of twenty-one.

Students were becoming antsy. They wanted a tale that would be worthy of delaying their snack time by multiple minutes. What they had heard thus far wasn't it. Two students—Billy Jane and Terry Cox —considered railroading this reading because they believed, if multiple students objected to this narrative event, their teacher would scrap it altogether. Elijah, everyone's go-to sacrificial lamb, reminded the two objectors via whisper that they might get away from hearing the story, but it could result in the complete cancellation of snack time. This possibility was real and not worth anyone's time.

Sensing that she was losing her crowd, Barbara skipped ahead multiple paragraphs to what she considered juicy material.

"Erica realized that thirty-six years of marriage was enough. She knew something had to be done and fast. Divorce was in her immediate future. But the paperwork and lawyer expenses made her reconsider. No, she wouldn't divorce the man she thought she loved. She would, after developing a sound plan, kill him."

The room went silent. The students turned their heads to check in with others to confirm that they heard what they all thought they heard. Barbara continued.

"Poison his morning coffee? No. This would leave a trace. Stab him with a

knife? No. There would be too much blood, and she would have to find the perfect hiding place for the weapon. Push him down the stairwell? No. It could be too hard to convince the cops that it was an accident."

The kids forgot about snack time altogether; they hung on her every word like they had their first taste of drugs and couldn't wait for their teacher—the powerful provider of disturbing juice— to hear what was going to happen next.

William chimed in. "I know what method the Erica character's going to use." The crowd turned on him instantly. "Don't you dare spoil it, or I'll—"

Mrs. Fredricks closed the notebook again, but this time she left her index finger in the middle of the page, having full confidence that she would finish this story even if a shooter busted into the room and started firing bullets at will. The students went quiet again.

Mrs. Fredericks took a deep breath. She reveled in this moment. She was at the ending.

"The only method available to Erica resided in the bedroom. Since her husband had two heart-related scares in the past two years, she knew that she could use this to her advantage. She waited for him to get into bed. Once he did, he grabbed a mystery novel off the nightstand and read what he could until his eyes convinced him that it was nighty-night time. Erica knew that this was her time to act. Outweighing his slight frame by more than forty-six pounds, Erica crawled across the bed and sat on his chest. His eyes went wide at this maneuver. Initially, he thought it was a joke. But her expression told a different story. He tried to get her to stop. He begged her to stop. He tried to nudge her gently backward, still clinging to some optimistic notion that this was a prank they would chuckle about in the morning. Erica remained in place and smothered his face with a pillow that was re-gifted to her by his insufferable mother. The life went out of her husband shortly after that, and all she could do upon his expiration date was laugh."

Mrs. Fredericks closed her notebook and tucked it under her stool.

"Everyone can get their snack now."

No one said a word during snack time, which was extremely rare. The silence was not a by-product of their teacher's writing ability. It was eerie and dark, yes. However, the students remained silent because their teacher, a woman who claimed that she was their moral guide daily, had shared a twisted story that might actually be true.

The bell rang in the middle of snack time. Mrs. Fredericks hadn't prepared the students for this occurrence. This resulted in students running around like chickens with their heads cut off. If one was counting, the collision tally might have exceeded six.

Students waited in the hallway for Mrs. Fredericks to escort them to their next destination. Annoyed, she delivered a harsh reminder: "You may walk to Art on your own! How else are you going to get ready for the fifth grade?"

All of them vanished but one. As Mrs. Fredericks massaged her temples and popped an Advil at her desk, Elijah returned to the classroom.

"Mr. Wells won't be happy with you, and I'm not giving you a pass."

"That's okay," Elijah said.

"What is it, kiddo? This is my free period."

"The teacher in the story was you."

"The teacher's name was Erica."

"You could've changed it. Besides, your husband died this year."

"...You going to rat me out?"

A mammoth silence took over the room. Elijah eyed Mrs. Fredericks; she eyed him back.

"That method...works?

Uh oh, thought Mrs. Fredericks. She knew her tale would entertain students. She knew it would scare, or even shock them. She did not consider the possibility of it inspiring one.

"I understand that you have yourselves a situation at home. But taking another's life is never the answer."

This was the response that should have left her chapped lips. Instead, six words came out.

"That method did wonders for me."

RED COUCH

THERE WERE two players in the story. Both of them were middle-aged females, and both of them needed to resolve an urgent matter.

Lynn Vanderloo didn't suffer from empty nest syndrome. That typically happens to parents who have children that head off to their first year of college. Lynn's layabout son started college at Salem State five years ago and, at present, was only a little more than a third of the way through his "undecided" degree. Sick and tired of shelling out money for a horrific grade point average, Lynn confronted her son one night.

"You're dropping out and getting a job, or you're taking out loans to pay for your education."

Her son disliked both choices. But he hated arguing with his mother more. She paid for everything in his life. It was high time he accepted this fact and made a decision that would benefit her future.

Through a series of mumbles, he said, "If I got a full-time thing, wouldja help me get, like, an apartment?"

Lynn overlooked this as a possibility since her son had a lengthy history of indecision. Even though this would cost her, she considered the money to be a worthier investment. He, God love him, would be gone from her living space. She would get her identity back!

"I'll secure a place for you and take care of the first month's rent, but it is your job from there on out to handle the monthly payments."

There was a deafening silence. Lynn understood that her son felt suffocated under this type of pressure. She didn't care. She had to be tough on him, or else he would learn nothing throughout his life. He stroked his sandy beard that looked like he was a member of a ZZ Top cover band.

"O—kay."

Four days later—Lynn wanted to get the show on the road—she secured a studio apartment above an electronics store that amounted to a debatable four-hundred and thirty-five square feet. When the realtor informed Lynn that he would be showing the unit to another client in thirty minutes, she took action.

"I'll take it. Cancel that appointment."

While the realtor drew up the paperwork, Lynn took a drive

around the city. She had her son's 2005 Ford Ranger. She took it after her Toyota Corolla failed to start. For a few seconds, she thought of canceling her appointment with the realtor. But ridding herself of her son and capturing her freedom was much more important than resolving some inexplicable and untimely car issue.

By happenstance, Lynn passed a red couch seemingly abandoned by the owner of a mustard colonial. A blank white sign lay on the ground. She put the truck in reverse, even though the orange marker appeared to be on neutral, and backed into the driveway.

Lynn stepped out of the parked truck and walked over to the white sign. She flipped it over. It read "Free." She rested it atop the couch. After doing so, she looked at the house's bay window and found three pairs of eyes aimed at her. A white Persian cat gave her a dismissive look; a brown Portuguese Water Dog sized her up with wide-eyed amazement; a severe-looking woman's intense eyes appeared to say, "Yes, dummy. That couch is free."

Unsure of how to proceed, Lynn waited for the homeowner to make a move. This couch was practically in mint condition. She would be a certifiable fool not to walk away with a free piece of furniture. Her question, the only one worth asking, would not be answered truthfully by the owner of the couch.

Samantha Deavers didn't suffer fools gladly; she wondered why this idiot didn't take the couch and go. The sign made everything clear. The couch wasn't that heavy. The visitor could have easily tipped one end into the bed of the rusty truck and then pushed it as far as it would allow. But no. She stood there like a calm invader.

Alas, Samantha exited her home and descended the steep lawn to complete the transaction.

"Hello there!" the visitor screamed.

Not one for shouters, Samantha remained quiet until she stood less than five feet away from this pushy customer.

"There a problem?" Samantha asked.

"I don't know. Is there?"

Lynn laughed at her question. Samantha stared at her blankly, hoping this reaction would expedite and end their unplanned encounter. Lynn motioned to the couch in an overdramatic manner.

"Nobody gives away a couch this nice."

"Don't judge a book by its cover."

Samantha bent down and tugged on the red fabric. It stretched. She lifted a portion of the corner to reveal the couch's real design: a fall setting with leaves, acorns, squirrels, and flowers.

"It was my father's. If I didn't cover it, no one would want it."

Lynn laughed—too hard for Samantha's liking—and immediately morphed into a serious tone.

"It's for my son's new apartment."

"He a clean freak?"

"I wish."

"They sell different colors if he doesn't like red."

"He loves red."

"Then this, my dear, is a no-brainer."

Samantha and Lynn lifted and guided the couch into the back of the pickup. Lynn couldn't hide her joy; Samantha worked hard to hide hers.

"It's too late for you to take it back," Lynn stated.

"That it is."

"I'm going to drive off now."

"I won't stop you."

Lynn climbed out of the bed of the truck and lost her footing. Samantha prevented her from hitting the pavement.

"Oh, thank you. I really can't give you twenty bucks?"

"You cannot."

"My son's going to be so happy. He's got this enormous movie poster of *The Shining*. The red on the poster is the perfect match for this."

"I have a busy day ahead of me."

"Oh, right. Sorry. I do too. Even though I am not acting like it. Have a great day."

"Do the same."

Lynn drove away from the house. Her truck bounced as it went over a speed table; the red couch nearly fell out. Samantha watched her go.

When Lynn's truck vanished from sight, Samantha pondered the events from the last twenty-four hours. At five p.m., she set a card on the kitchen table with a present next to it. An hour later, she finished frosting a carrot cake—hubby's favorite—and then placed it into the refrigerator. Minutes away from seven, she set the dining room table with tan placemats and burnt orange napkins. By seven-thirty-five, she served her husband a tomahawk steak (the kind he never tried before) with a side of fingerling potatoes, broccoli, and field greens lightly covered with Raspberry Balsamic Vinaigrette. Throughout the meal, he said less than eight words, all of which related to accepting a second plate or replying to a question about how something was cooked or tasted. Given her elaborate efforts to honor the occasion, she was taken aback by his failure to praise them. He vacated the table, removed his oil-covered work shirt, left it on the chair he used, and then headed for the shower. It was a game of chicken. Did he remember their anniversary or not?

Before joining her in the living room, he stopped in front of the card and foil-wrapped present.

"Who's that for?"

"Not me," Samantha teased.

He shoved the card aside and directed his attention to the gift. He tore the foil off in one go.

"'Spensive one."

"Yes, it was."

He joined her on the couch. In a fog, Samantha rolled a gold object between her hands while a Waspy commentator warned the nation about cancel culture on the TV.

All Samantha wanted was acknowledgment. All Samantha wanted was to hear "Happy Anniversary" from the man her parents objected to her marrying. All Samantha got was silence.

Her husband opened the bottle of bourbon with his unusually strong teeth, spit aside the cap, and took a superhuman swig. He put the bottle down and burped. This lack of care and class enraged her.

Instead of using words, which always got her nowhere with Captain Taciturn, she opted for the physical approach. She opened her right palm wide for him to see. Her husband paid the Japanese letter opener zero mind. She jammed it into his jugular and forced his face down. A portion of his blood spurt into Samantha's eyes; the rest soaked into the couch.

By ten p.m., her husband was dead. She wrapped his body in their old pool cover and dragged him to the garage through the back entrance. She loaded him into the trunk of her Chevy Impala.

By midnight, Samantha dumped his lifeless body in a nearby hiking trail that was notorious for its bear sightings. She removed four packages of potent suet from her coat pockets and placed them around her husband. If the bears didn't consume him throughout the night, something more vicious would.

At nine the next morning, she entered Wal-Mart with the sole intention of finding a slipcover that wouldn't attract attention. At ten a.m., she removed a piece of printing paper from her office and wrote, in purple sharpie, the word "FREE" in all caps.

With the couch, or item loaded with most of the criminal evidence, removed from the equation, all Samantha had to do was lead a normal life and be prepared with a set of perfect lies in case the cops ever visited her.

There were two players in this story. Both of them were middle-aged females, and both of them had resolved an urgent matter.

TAUNT THAT WITCH

THERE WAS nothing unusual about Talulah's skating route. She always took the same shortcut home through the paved walkway in the cemetery. However, today presented a variable: a steaming pile of dog crap in the middle of her path. She noticed it at the last second, swerved overdramatically, and went right to the ground. While her upper half benefitted from the soft, wet grass, her lower half greeted the pavement with tremendous force.

Talulah rolled over and sat up. She winced in pain. From her ankles to her kneecaps, there were bits of gravel embedded into her pale skin. Her mother had yelled at her that morning for wearing shorts. But the TV weather girl, dressed like she was ready for a racy club, informed the Salem locals that it would be a hot one for October.

Talulah tried to stand, but realized that she needed an additional moment to get her bearings. She scanned the cemetery. No activity. Thankfully no one had witnessed her epic fall. Or so she thought. Someone could have recorded it without her knowledge. By dinner-time, she could be on YouTube! It wasn't her fault. An entitled person didn't care enough to clean up their dog's doo-doo, and they didn't care enough about this sensitive environment—the land of the deceased—to keep it clean as multiple signs requested of its visitors.

Talulah's eyes landed on the headstone in front of her. Even though she didn't believe in ghosts, she got the immediate creeps. Maisie May, a supposed witch from the 1700s, was the town specter that haunted those that dared to say her name three times, those that dared to speak or think negatively about her, and those that vandalized her grave. The only reason Talulah knew all this was because her teachers, from middle school until her current standing as a high school sophomore, played up the legend for all it was worth during the week leading up to Halloween.

Talulah immediately noticed that the grass in front of the headstone was disturbed. She pushed the dirt and grass together in a feeble attempt to make it look better.

"Relax, Maisie May. It wasn't on purpose." Then, under her breath, she added, "Stupid witch." Talulah laughed and quickly regretted it.

She didn't believe in the legend or that this deceased woman could harm people in the present. Regardless, she felt uneasy speaking disrespectfully to a dead being, and a legendary one at that.

Talulah stood up, massaged her knees and shins, and then put her longboard at her feet. She put her left foot on the front of the board and pedaled with her right. She let her right foot join the left, and she rode, like she did Monday through Friday, down the serpentine path that ended at the one-hundred-yard mark and led, via a wooded area, to the backyard of her neighbors' home.

Less than ten seconds down the hill, Talulah recognized one problem: she was going too fast. Her familiarity with the hill's descent and its random turns allowed her to remain on the board. But something didn't feel right, and she couldn't quite put her finger on it. When she lowered her right foot off the board in an attempt to use it as a brake, it was forced back next to her left foot. Not good. She tried to hop off the board entirely, but her body, held in place by an invisible force, wouldn't go anywhere.

Talulah screamed for help. She tried to pivot the board in the direction of a grassy area. If she were going to lose control, she would find a soft place to land. But she couldn't alter the direction of the board either. Someone else was in charge, and she was at their mercy. What was happening?!

Seconds later, Talulah propelled forward, face first, into a *Please Clean Up After Your Pet* sign. She sat up and spit out a large amount of blood. It wasn't her first fall; it wouldn't be her last. "Is that all you got, Maisie?"

Talulah propped herself up with the longboard and looked back in the direction of the headstones. All was quiet and peaceful. "Who believes in witches anyway?" She chuckled and then added, "No one."

Talulah turned towards the path that led home. Suddenly, she stumbled backward in fright. A woman wearing black garb from head to toe stood before her. "Hello, Talulah."

Talulah's stomach dropped. Before she could ask how the mysterious woman knew her name, she was attacked.

ADAM AND SUTTON

AFTER SUTTON SET another record for silence, Adam took a chance at dialogue when he noticed a road sign of particular interest.

"Look at the Mass Pike sign! That's picture-worthy."

Sutton didn't react at all. Who cared about a stupid sign with a pilgrim's hat on it? No one but her dad.

"Perhaps you can snap one on the way back." Her silence suggested that this wasn't likely. "Up for Fuddrucker's? We have a little time to kill. Lord knows I could use a burger or two."

Adam chuckled. His put-on enthusiasm for everything fell on Sutton's deaf ears. She wished he would shut the hell up. He was like one of those horrible substitute teachers that tried, throughout a class period, to be relatable. No wonder he couldn't land dates or get a better job; he had next to no personality.

"Used to go there after all my Little League games. You haven't lived till you've tried a Fuddrucker's burg—"

"Not hungry."

"Or we could stop at the Witch House. Pretty sure there's a wax museum in that area as well. Either one of those'd be cool, no?"

"What-ever."

Adam hated this response from anyone. It especially ticked him off when it was delivered by his daughter. He was doing everything in his power to please her and she failed to acknowledge it. *At least acknowledge my damn effort*, he thought.

One minute later, it was back to total silence. While it pained Adam to endure such treatment, he pushed himself to tolerate it because he had invited Sutton to Salem under false pretenses. He had always been transparent with her about every single development in his life. But this was an exception. He had an ace up his sleeve that was bound to make her react. Had he told her the reason for the trip prior to getting in the truck, they never would have left their home in Connecticut.

Sutton had two modes: one of legendary silence (reserved mostly for her father), which forced her social partner to ramble on before they surrendered; her other mode, heavily verbal, was reserved for the people that she detested. While her hatred list was a mile long, no one ranked higher than that of Terry Dennis.

Adam knew this to be the case, which was why he was beyond concerned that, within the hour, they were not heading to a hotel (as promised) but to a colonial home where her arch-rival was waiting.

CRUNCHY BITS

HIS BUSINESS WASN'T OPEN a month before it had the townsfolk buzzing. He certainly had his reasons for opening *Your Next Candy Shoppe*; however, making a profit wasn't one of them.

That was for him to know and the customers to find out.

William Smith was a rather boring man. Even he would agree with the assessment given to him as a teenager. He was slim, balding, and bespectacled. Looks aside, there wasn't much of a personality present either. He spoke in a low and unclear voice that forced most to make him repeat himself. This always ticked him off because he was speaking as clearly as he could. Sometimes he wanted to yell, "Open your ears!"

The candy shoppe idea came to him about a year back. Dragged to Salem by his insufferable mother—who was in the later stages of Parkinson's disease by the way—she had forced William to take her to this and that tour. Her tremors usually impacted her mobility so much that she would have to take breaks every fifteen minutes. This was not the case in Salem. She moved around like she was only just diagnosed with her disease. Usually wearing a wicked disposition (or what the kids would call "resting bitch face"), Barbara Smith beamed from ear to ear.

"C'mon! If we hurry through this Nightmare Gallery thing, we can make it to the Witch Museum next."

William was amused by her excitement because, well, she was a person that rarely displayed it. So, he complied with her every wish. It wasn't until the day neared its end that ole Barbara returned to the surface and made William regret signing up for this trip.

With apple poison martini in her shaky hand, Barbara scanned the crowded tequila bar, dismissed a youthful bartender for showing off her large bust, and then set her eyes on her 41-year-old son. There was no food in front of him. Only a glass of water.

"You're such a loser. It makes me sick!"

William was caught off-guard by her sneak attack. He drove her here. He paid for everything: food, gas, medicine, and tacky alcohol.

"Are you ever going to do something with your life? One thing? Are you? Find a woman? Find a man, for all I care. You're pathetic. So pathetic, it makes me want to drink two more of these. No. Four more. I don't care if it prevents my meds from working. The sight of you, the energy of you, makes me want to die. Kill me, would you? Would you kill me and then do something with your life?"

Surprisingly, William did both.

The killing of his mother was easier than he imagined. It truly was. The process of doing it was thrilling, and the return to regular life was seamless. He expected a high level of guilt to overtake his mind, but it never did. This shocked him. He had watched tons of *Dateline* episodes, which, more times than not, led to someone spilling the beans about their heinous acts because they regretted what they did.

Not William. He regretted nothing. The act of removing his mother from this world made him want to kill as many people as possible.

So, that's what he did.

In less than seven months—until the time he relocated here five weeks ago—William had killed four people. He wasn't thrilled with the number. He wanted it to be much higher, but the killing of others wasn't the lengthy part. It was in the dismemberment of their bodies.

The back room at *Your Next Candy Shoppe* became the place for body part removal. He would certainly concede that this location increased the odds of him getting caught. But he didn't care about getting caught. The notion of hiding such terrible deeds in plain sight amused him.

His highest level of amusement came from two visitors: a building inspector and a street clothes cop. The former was a blonde woman of Polish descent. She marched around his establishment and took notes as if no one else was in the room with her. Little did she know that personality-less William had cut the arms and legs off a Middle Eastern construction worker fifty minutes prior.

He wondered if he'd missed a bloodstain. He didn't care though. He could just kill Joanna Borkowski if she noticed anything amiss. But it wasn't, and she didn't. She finished writing her notes, delivered a rapid smile, and then said "Good luck" as she vacated the premises.

While the curvaceous inspector certainly kept William stimulated, it was the street clothes cop that turned him on like no other. The cop, a new hire six months ago, would pop in daily to purchase treats for his pregnant wife. The baby was due in three months. William pretended to care about the baby. The truth of the matter was he wanted a few minutes alone with it to prevent it from having an existence.

Unfortunately, he never encountered the baby. Only the cop. Slowly but surely, he learned that the man's name was Kenneth Stead. He looked like most cops with one exception: he had a burgundy birthmark that started at his right cheek and curved down towards his sharp jaw. If William ended his life, he would begin at the origin point of said birthmark. William had no interest in killing Kenneth, however. It was more amusing to let him in and out of the store with the murder energy around them.

Kenneth's desired treats were called Crunchy Bits. Kenneth snagged a few from a *Free Sample* basket near the register station on William's grand opening. Kenneth ignored that they were covered in chocolate and put them into his coat pocket as if he were putting aside milk bones for his dog. When William shared this observation, Kenneth replied in a deadpan manner:

"My wife is a bit of a dog."

The men broke into hoots of laughter. William hadn't laughed that hard since he had sealed his mother's exit from this earth.

This moment meant so much to William that he decided he would turn himself in to Kenneth—admit every murder and every single detail—when someone either started to inquire about the treats' ingredients, or he became bored with his new status quo.

Neither path scared him. He had reached an elevated mental state. Most people didn't accomplish what he did, nor did they arrive at a mental place where death, health, and jail were meaningless.

He had taken the lives of sixteen people in fifteen months of business. Fourteen of said sixteen were dismembered, mixed in with the chocolate, nuts, and caramel to create the customers' favorite treat. They couldn't get enough. William would pretend to sell out weekly to keep the demand high. There was one other benefit to this lie: he earned more time to kill and dismember.

On the eve of Halloween, William hacked off the fingers of an older woman. She'd popped into the store to ask for directions, and when William replied with his best guess, the woman ordered him to speak up. He told her he was speaking up. Had she let it go, she would still be breathing. But she went all-in on William and stated that he would never run a successful business shop if he mumbled regularly. He unplugged and then heaved his espresso machine at her. It was a direct hit to her temple.

It only took him twelve minutes to drag the body into the back-room and then clean-slash-disinfect the kill scene. Three minutes later, however, Kenneth arrived. And his energy seemed different than usual. Had he caught William in the act while he was parked across the street?

"I tell you we got a new pooch?"

"You get rid of the old one?" William asked.

"Oh. Sorry. It's our first one."

"Breed?"

"Australian Shepherd."

"Supposed to be smart dogs."

"Supposed to be."

"Thought you were having a real baby?"

"She *lost* it. Hence, the dog."

William knew this was the part where a normal person would apologize, where one would wax poetic about how precious life was and that it can forever humble people. Instead, he handed over a fresh batch of chocolate-covered pretzels. Kenneth smirked and then held one near his mouth. He had never done this before. William watched with intense anticipation.

Kenneth pointed the pretzel at him, and then spoke:

"Funny thing about dogs..."

William's brain instantly traveled to a place that made him consider what made dogs funny, and he came up with nil.

"They're not supposed to have chocolate. I grew up hearing this.

I've told my wife this. And still, she gave him a piece. Right in front of my face. But guess what the dog did? He spit it out. Even though they're not supposed to eat it, dogs will eat anything. Any-thing you put in front of them. Which made me approach—at first, to prevent him from eating something that could kill him, and then to see why he would turn down such a delicious treat. That's when I found these."

Bits of bone rested in Kenneth's right hand. William didn't glance at them. Instead, he sat on the stool behind the treat counter.

"Can you say it again?"

"Say what again?" asked Kenneth.

"C'mon. You know."

Kenneth didn't. William stood up from the stool and offered his popular treats.

"Put 'em in your pocket. Then I'll say it's like you're putting them away for your dog. And you'll go…

William waited. Kenneth did not and would not oblige.

"You'll go, 'My wife is a bit of a dog!'"

William cracked up. Kenneth stared at him. Their shared moment in the past lost all of its luster. William's face turned bright red. To account for his sudden rage, he shoved the treats into his mouth, chewed for the world to see, and then choked to death on the linoleum floor.

Kenneth didn't help him. It wasn't because he thought William should meet his maker. He simply froze. He stood there like a statue and pondered how this ordinary man had used this quaint location as a crime scene. He pondered why he hadn't seen all this before. He pondered why he became a cop. He pondered if he should remain one. He pondered why he'd married his wife. He pondered why he tried to have a baby with her. He pondered why he would let that stupid dog serve as some replacement baby. He pondered if he, too, could get rid of them in the manner that William had.

When his pondering stopped, he grabbed his walkie and called for assistance.

HOMAGE

I HAD A TYPICAL AMERICAN UPBRINGING. My father ignored me. My mother rode my ass frequently and never dished out a compliment. My younger sister stole all of the attention when she arrived four years after me. My younger brother died in a freakish pool accident before he could get his claws into my psyche. The only survivor left to inflict mental damage was my youngest sister. She wasn't a bother to me anymore, however. We ceased all communication years ago.

I tried to reflect on these factors since I couldn't afford a shrink, let alone convince myself to go to one. My reflection was interrupted by a yapping dog three homes over. I took a picture of it three nights ago and compared it to dog photos on Google. It was a Jack Russell terrier. Aside from photos, I learned that this breed produced some of the smartest dogs on the planet. I couldn't deduce whether or not it was intelligent; what I could grasp was that it didn't shut up. It was as if somebody shoved a new battery into its back and allowed it to test out its barking capabilities at all hours of the night.

The dog reminded me of my mother. I had to hurt it as soon as possible. I located my father's handgun. It was where he always left it: in the cabinet below the bathroom sink behind the titty mags. My father had more guns, but this one remained in that location if an intruder prevented him from reaching the main stash.

I checked the chamber; it was fully loaded. It was go time. I stood in place and listened. The dog barked incessantly. Didn't he need a break? How could he keep this up?

I paused in front of a full-length mirror. I needed to remove my light-colored clothes.

Dressed in black from head to toe, I snuck into the backyard of the Hendersons, a family of conservatives. The motion detector blasted light into my eyes; I ducked behind a newly constructed shed that displayed a green "Juan Deere" sign. This family liked to announce their racist tendencies, but they did not care, one way or another, about a psychotic dog.

I poked my head out from behind the shed and stared into their living room window. It was evident why they didn't care about the dog. Fox News played on the television. Those commentators shouted so much that it overpowered any background noise. This made it easier for me to reach the wooden fence that stood mere feet away from the noisy culprit.

I removed the handgun from my waist and moved towards the fence. It was higher than I thought. I adapted to its dimensions, stood on my tippy-toes, and fired one, two, three shots.

I thought about sending the powers-that-be at Fox News a thank you letter because no one inside the Henderson home moved an inch. Unfortunately, multiple bodies emerged from the dog's home. I boogied on out of there.

I ran to my bathroom and locked the door. I put my father's handgun in its usual place and sat in the lime-colored bathtub. I figured the cops would enter my home forcefully within the hour, so I steeled myself for the possibility that this would be my last night in the comforts of home.

I woke six hours later, confused about my surroundings. I raised my head quickly and hit my forehead against the tub spout. Blood trickled past my right eye and curved past my lips. I sat up, crawled out of the tub, and checked the condition of my face in the mirror. I was ghastly. It was so goddamn beautiful.

I opened the front door and headed outside to retrieve the morning news. I expected a nondescript van to be parked across the street so they could monitor my every move. Everything was quiet.

I got away with murdering that stupid dog. I felt like Son of Sam. Well, I couldn't be the son. I would have to refer to myself as the Daughter of Sam. But there wasn't a Sam in the picture, which made this idea unlikely to come to fruition.

I wondered what else I could get away with. Had my parents been alive, I would have murdered them today. After I offed the dog, I knew I possessed the mental capacity to eliminate those ungrateful bastards.

I was at a mental crossroads. If I could remove a dog from this world, why couldn't I remove a few humans?

As if I tasted a drink officially made for me, I committed to becoming a serial killer. I had nothing better to do. Before I picked my first victim, I wrote a poem to convey my thoughts about kill number one. This wasn't necessary, but if I intended to become the new age Daughter of Sam, I had to leave behind writing proof that made me appear off my rocker.

I could have drafted a letter directed at somebody, but I didn't know anyone important. The result, devoid of corrections, was as follows:

The pup pup pup
Had to shut up
So after a single cerveza
I made my wayza
Over to his home
And watched his barks of foam
I fired a pop pop pop
There was never a cop
Oh, what a strange sight
Look at all my might

I shoved the poem aside, hoping to use it on a rainy day or allowing it to be found by a cop when the city of Salem realized they had a serial killer in their midst.

Despite having the entire day ahead of me, I went to sleep for a few hours. I wasn't nervous or ashamed of my act; I didn't get quality sleep in the tub. A small part of me wondered if I went to sleep in an attempt to drown out the thoughts of my latest career plan.

When I awoke, I still had the desire to kill. Or at least I wasn't repelled by the notion. It felt like my calling had arrived. Had that intelligent dog not been a royal nuisance, I would have been the same old woman. I had to thank him.

"Thanks, pup. Wherever you are," I said as if he were in the kitchen with me. I wasn't going crazy. I felt alive for the first time in my life, and I needed to thank somebody.

When nighttime arrived, I journeyed through the city. There were so many people out and about since it was October, or as my father claimed, "The month of the dang tourists." I considered blasting a person in the cobblestone area near the Peabody Essex Museum, but there were too many people around. I could end someone's life with a single witness around; however, I couldn't do so with hundreds of witnesses around.

I had a reputation to start. Killings in crowds would come later. How much later depended on my knack for being a killer of humans.

The next evening, I strolled through Salem Common. I decided that my first murder, and all subsequent ones, would occur in or around this famous area. The early October night gave me one favor: a torrential downpour. It kept a large portion of the tourists and locals indoors; this lowered the number of witnesses. If there was a God, she was clearly on my side here.

I stood under an awning near Skeleton Tavern. I smoked a cigarette and watched various people try to escape the rain. The rain came down with such force that it impacted my visibility. I needed a better location and fast.

I stumbled upon the entranceway of Museum Place Parking Garage on New Liberty Street. There was a heavyset man with glasses inside an office. I checked him out. He was wide-awake and very focused on monitoring the activity of this garage. I wondered if an alternate location would be necessary; however, I realized that I didn't have an umbrella. This gave me the excuse I needed. I raised the collar of my dark blue windbreaker over my head and hurried for the stairwell. I climbed a few levels and waited. I looked up and around, making sure not to miss a beat. There were no cameras. I waited. The stairwell smelled like piss and semen. I hoped that it was the result of one person; I feared that it was a perverted party's contributions.

I held my breath for as long as I could. Then I heard it. Footsteps. It sounded like boots or heels. No, boots were louder. This had to be a woman!

I got ready. I blocked out the horrific smells, wiped the sweat from my brow, and fought back a sneeze.

The heels turned the corner. I noticed a red hat and a lime jacket first. Then a pale face covered by matted brown hair. Her right hand came out of her pocket and reached for the door to B3.

I whistled. She turned. I fired my gun. The bullet ripped through her neck. She fell like a ton of bricks. I stood over her and grinned. A pool of blood spread below her body. I spun her over so I could remove her jacket and hat. Donning those, I passed the man in the office. His eyes were glued to the sports section of a local paper.

I slept like a baby that night. Truthfully, I thought I would have the opposite experience. But the thrill of killing that seemingly faceless woman provided even more satisfaction than that nuisance of a dog.

Less because I was bloodthirsty and more because I was restless that the cops would catch me, I committed to another kill the next night. Furthermore, no one would make a connection between the dog and the woman. I had to do it for them by adding bodies to the land known for its witches.

Over the next four evenings, the local authorities had their work cut out for them. I dropped an elderly man with two rounds in front of Sam's café on Monday; I sat on a bench in Salem Common on Tuesday and blasted a jogging teenager whose dumb smile suggested she actually loved running; I surprised a lesbian couple out for a stroll along Salem Harbor with a pair of bullets to their temples on Wednesday; and, lastly, on Thursday, I ended the existence of a Spanish woman who exited City Hall with a box of files that caused her to trip on the stairwell. The files went everywhere. I helped her pick them up. After she thanked me, I fired rounds into both of her hefty breasts.

The weekend edition of various newspapers tabbed me "The Salem Common Killer" or "The Killer of Essex." While both names were rather catchy, I was disappointed that nobody linked me to the dog. For this reason, I drafted a disturbing letter with many typos (because killers do that on purpose). When I reached the end of the message, I added the following for effect:

Always yours,
Daughter of Sam

I rummaged the house for a stamp and envelope; I only found the former. I would have to pay a visit to CVS tomorrow.

On Friday evening, I waited in line with a box of ramen, a can of Monster, a package of red pens, and a box of envelopes. I intended to use red ink outside of every envelope I sent to police or news stations.

The line barely moved because an African American teen contested the total price of his candy haul. The aging cashier with thick glasses and cane came out from behind the counter to examine the yellow sale tags that hung in front of the candy section.

"Well, whaddya know? Yer right."

The teen held his ground and turned to eyeball me and the others waiting as if to say, "Stop giving me your dirty looks. It was all worth it." The total on the register screen changed dramatically. The teen paid and left in a huff.

I wanted to blow the little runt's brains out. I had daddy's gun with me. I could do it. But I had a more pressing matter, which was buying these damn envelopes to inform the locals and state of Massachusetts whom they were presently dealing with.

I left CVS six minutes later. I planned on heading home, but I noticed that the African American teen was contesting yet another price at an outdoor kiosk. I wanted to wring his neck. Was he a savvy shopper or a game player?

I watched him convince yet another business that he was in the right. It sickened me. He deserved a bullet. I didn't have to kill him, but I did need to send him a message.

He headed down the cobblestone street and swung a right towards City Hall. I looked ahead and noticed that no one was on either side of the street. It was the perfect opportunity. When he paused to check his phone outside of Honey Dew Donuts, I charged him with gun drawn, strictly intending to put a bullet in his leg. He whipped around suddenly, wrestled the gun away from me, and fired a round into my abdomen.

Overcome with shock, I asked him how he knew that I was coming.

"Saw yo reflection in the mirror."

I nodded to take ownership of my error. I was losing blood fast.

"Call the cops?"

"Yer lucky I don't cap y'again."

He was correct. I was lucky he didn't cap me again. But the world had to know my desired moniker, and if I perished on this-here sidewalk, my work would have all been for nothing.

"Do me…

"I don't do old broads."

"…a favor."

"Why would I do you a fava?"

"I'm the…one…that…

His impatience grew. He turned to leave. I couldn't bear it. I fought to get the words out. It was too difficult, though. Instead, I remembered that my note, the one that announced my identity, was in my pocket. I removed it and held it out for him.

"Dat important?" he asked.

I nodded with a hopeful smile. He smiled back, and then he drew an orange lighter from his ripped jeans. He lit the paper on fire and watched as my expression shifted to hopelessness.

"Well, it ain't important no more."

I laughed. He laughed. Less than a minute later, I was dead. The only written evidence in my home was a poem about a dead dog. My final thought was, "Do the cops have enough evidence to mark me as the town's serial killer, or will they write me off as a dog killer and nothing more?"

STALKER 101

HENNA GILLESPIE OR MACKENZIE WELTON?

That one choice would dictate his fate.

Three weeks ago, Harold Roberts' world came crashing down when his mother collapsed in the kitchen, holding the porcelain teakettle given to her at a real estate function by a coworker she adamantly disliked.

Short of a minor miracle, the kettle remained in perfect condition after the fall. Harold's mother, however, was an entirely different story. She was one hundred percent dead.

The instant passing took the breath right out of Harold. He knew that it was more likely than not that parents leave this earth before their children. He just thought he would have more time to prepare for it mentally. His mother, a realtor with next to no companions, was diagnosed with early Alzheimer's three weeks prior. That was how he thought she would go. That is how she should have gone. Not by a sudden aneurysm.

But here was Harold, sitting alone in the home he had been in since birth. He had no clue what the future held because he never did anything to direct its course. Nope. Not a single thing.

Even though a stinkbug was doing its best to hold his attention, he could not shake the fact that he owned a pathetic bio that was worthy of everyone's ridicule. He took a blue pen to a yellow notepad to emphasize his current thought and wrote HAROLD'S LIFE on the top. Underneath, he wrote the following:

-I never married.

-I never had sex.

-I never had a date of any kind.

-I never had alcohol.

-I never did drugs.

-I never left the state.

-I never got a promotion.

-I never got a new car.

-I never fixed a car.

-I never had my own place.

-I never exercised (except when I was a kid in P.E. class).

-I never went to the doctor (after being checked out by grumpy nurses in schools).

-I never went on a diet.

-I never used a weapon.

-I never committed a crime.

Harold paused here to examine the list. Even he found it curious why he would include the bit about no criminal record. But it wasn't as if anyone but him would see this list.

In a rare moment of motivation, Harold sprung his 400-plus pound body out of the chair and thwacked the stink bug with the back of the yellow note pad. It slid down the mustard refrigerator and oozed its way into expiration. Harold laughed and snagged his jacket off a coat rack that appeared as if it would fall at any second.

Less than one hour later, Harold left the state of Massachusetts and entered New Hampshire. He pulled over immediately because he had no idea where to go, nor what to do. He wished he had his yellow pad handy so he could cross "Never left the state" off his list. He didn't have to do something interesting in another state; he merely needed to prove he had the temerity to visit one. With a calmness he didn't usually display, Harold found his way back to his home state and returned to Salem.

Harold opened the freezer, intent on wolfing down the last ice cream sandwich. He refrained, however. Instead, he bent down, picked up the dead stinkbug, apologized for taking his life, and then flushed him down the nearby toilet.

Tuckered out from the drive, Harold took two steps into his bedroom and then backed out. His mother was gone now. Why would he still have to sleep in a queen bed? He wouldn't. He could take full ownership of his mother's king-sized one.

Harold entered his mother's bedroom. The smell of old saltines and damp towels hit him instantly. He made a snap decision to sleep in his bedroom tonight and then clean out her room in the morning.

Before he flipped off his Yoda nightlight, Harold grabbed his yellow pad. He ran his right index finger down the list and stopped.

He crossed out "Never had my own place." This bungalow had offi-cially become his own. How he used it would be totally up to him.

As a result of a client canceling at the last minute, Harold was booked for a physical with Norman Peterson the next morning. He knew nothing of the man aside from the fact that most of his coworkers trusted him.

Harold sat in the waiting room and realized, as if for the first time, that he needed to do something about his weight ASAP because the fat on his right and left legs hung over the arms of each vacant chair next to him.

He expected the doctor to be brutal in the way that his mother was. But Norman Peterson, a stocky man with broad shoulders, could not have been kinder. He waxed poetic about Harold having the courage to make an appointment even though he possessed a history of neglecting them.

"Harold…" he said.

It didn't come out like a question but a command that made Harold fidget.

"…tell me about this diet of yours."

Because the tone in Peterson's voice was anything but threatening, because Peterson was warm from the word "go" and because Peterson seemed like he gave a damn about the patients in general, Harold gave him the unadulterated truth.

"This is rather embarrassing, but…I eat one or two 'a those Jimmy Dean sandwiches from the box every morning. Usually with some OJ and a coupla cups of coffee."

"Cream and sugar?" asked Peterson.

"Sugar and some 'a that CoffeeMate stuff. Y'know? The flavored cream?"

Peterson nodded. Beyond impressed by his doctor's prolonged lack of judgment in tone or expression, Harold moved on to his lunch habits.

"Lunch is one of two things. It's a salami and cheese sandwich with chips on the side, or it's macaroni and cheese from the box."

"Brand?"

"Velveeta."

Harold studied Peterson's face.

"I could prolly find a healthier brand, couldn't I?"

"Probably."

"Dinner's um... well, my mom usually made those, and she just passed."

"I am sorry for your loss."

Harold knew the man meant it, so he decided to go one step further regarding the truth-telling.

"My mom making me the meals has nothing to do with anything. I ate whatever she made at dinner and usually had seconds or thirds. Most times with dessert too."

"I appreciate your candor."

"You bring it outta me."

"So, Harold...tell me why you're here."

"Why am I here?"

Peterson nodded again and waited Harold out.

"I am here because... I am here because I know I need to make changes. Not making the goal to be that weight loss surgery y'see on them reality shows, but I need to alter some things to feel better. I think you're the person to tell me what to do."

"Tell me what you think you should do."

"Exercise some. More than some. A lot. Eat fruits. Veggies. Watch my calorie intake."

"What do you need me for?"

"What kind of exercises should I do? If I'm completely honest, I don't like the idea of gyms."

"You have a problem with walks?"

"I don't think so."

"I'll have you know that a walk, a daily walk, does a body good."

It was then and there where the doctor sealed Harold's fate. Of course, he didn't know it yet.

The very next day, Harold committed to a walking plan. Before he did so, he took a drive to the DSW in Beverly. The number of options scared him, so he deferred to the expertise of a bespectacled ginger teenager who insisted that God himself blessed any pair of Hoka One One's and that they were the only shoe that belonged on a human's feet.

Forty-five minutes later, Harold was about to take his first walk—at least for health and exercise reasons—toward Salem High School. His home on Endicott was 1.1 miles away. This meant Harold's new fitness plan would start at 2.2 miles daily. He didn't know if he could do it, but he had to try.

When Harold reached the high school, he nearly collapsed. He didn't think he could make it back to his home without the services of an Uber. *There was no shame in doing a mile walk*, Harold thought.

Harold dug into his shorts' pockets. All he found were his wallet and house keys. No phone. This meant no Uber. Harold would have to journey home in the manner that he had left it: by foot.

A group of teenagers cruised by him, all sporting unique face coverings. To save face, he pushed forward. He passed Colby Street. It was here that he started to see a series of lawn signs in succession that honored the accomplishments of the senior class of Salem High. This was the result of the pandemic that had gone global. Harold felt terrible for the students. He was no school lover, but to miss out on sports and proms and various ceremonies due to an invisible plague was downright inauspicious.

Harold studied the names and faces of each student he passed. He wondered what they would become in the future, and, if it was at all possible, that they could use this life-altering event to their advantage.

Now Henna Gillespie made him stop in his tracks. He knew his reaction was less about her future and more about her incredible looks. She had long, flowing brown hair that dipped below her cheekbones. To make matters worse, there was the hint of a large bust hiding behind her completely-appropriate-for-school-pictures blouse. Harold didn't like the feeling brought on by her picture, so he boogied past Heritage Drive.

Despite his distance from the picture, he could not shake its power. He realized he was repeating "Henna Gillespie" under his breath. If he had his phone handy, he would have typed her name into the Notes app.

He tried to think of a slew of mental distractions, but none of them worked. He noticed that the signs continued along, all the way towards Dalton Parkway. This fact made him focus on every sign hoping that new names would eject Henna from his mind. Momentarily, it worked.

That was until Harold became enraptured by a new girl: Mackenzie Welton. Whereas Henna's hair and apparent bust stole the center stage, it was Mackenzie's piercing blue eyes that seemed to command anyone that had the gall to stare at them long enough.

Harold was quite concerned now. He picked up his pace. All he had to do was clear Phelps Street, and he would be in the home stretch. But the names kept reverberating through his mind.

Henna Gillespie. Mackenzie Welton. Henna. Mackenzie. Gillespie. Welton.

Viewing the other signs didn't help! These two young girls transfixed him. And he knew they were still girls, even if their birthdays made them cross the eighteen-year-old-and-officially-legal line.

What was he thinking? What was he considering?

Females were not interested in Harold Roberts. Plain and simple. He needed to get these thoughts out of his mind and fast. The liquor store could help.

A Middle Eastern clerk waited for Harold to make a selection.

"I've never been wasted. What brand would make me forget things?"

The clerk smirked.

"Any-thing with the hundred proof."

"Okay, gimme two of those."

"Two of which?"

"That one with the pirate and that one with the turkey."

Harold uncapped both bottles the second he walked into his home, and he nearly barfed when he did. His newfound problem became how to consume these ghastly liquids. He typed each brand separately into Yahoo's search engine and then typed the word *mixers* alongside it. Both searches yielded results that relieved Harold. He could use ginger ale for the bourbon and Coke (even though he only had RC in the fridge) for the rum.

He went with the pirate brand right off the bat because he consumed cola like it was his job. He didn't understand portions or that he could make plenty of rum and cokes with the amount he purchased. Since this was the case, he dumped all of the bottle contents into a 25-ounce glass his mother bought in Cape Cod long before he was born.

Harold guzzled his concoction. It became apparent to him instantly that this was not how one is supposed to mix drinks. The booze overpowered the soda and resulted in a sickeningly sweet drink. But he had put worse things into his body. Therefore, he pressed on.

He thought he should be drunk by now. However, he had no comparison since he had never danced with the stuff.

Wait, oh wait, Harold thought. *Am I too fat? Do I have to drink both bottles tonight?*

He told himself 'no'. However, he still had the names of the girls in his head. Is he supposed to allow wait time for the liquor to do its magic?

That must be it, guessed Harold.

While he waited, Harold logged into an old Instagram account. He had two posts. He was following seven people. No one was following him.

He typed in his mother's username: FlowerMama67. Her page was still intact. He had no idea how to have it removed. Perhaps he would message the powers-that-be at Insta and ask them to suspend her page because of her lack of existence.

Instead of taking this action, he scrolled through her page. Every post was a flower from her garden over the years. He didn't understand the point of sharing such images with the world—her world being 14 followers—but he knew that this hobby proved to be cathartic days after her husband (and his father) died from a stroke in the dressing room of a JC Penny.

Harold checked the microwave clock. Only eleven minutes had passed, and the alcohol wasn't doing its job. He nearly signed out of Instagram, but his brain had other ideas. In the search engine, he typed Mackenzie Welton.

And there she was right at the top! The girl from the lawn sign! Harold looked left, right, and then behind him to make sure no one witnessed this act. He wished Norman Peterson were with him to calmly tell him that there were better ways to pursue the opposite sex. Harold clicked Mackenzie's profile icon and then closed his eyes. He was ashamed that he had taken it this far.

The page didn't load at first. Harold checked his Wi-Fi connection. Everything was good. A simple reload of the page thrust him into the visual world of a teenager he had no business creeping on.

But was his behavior creepy? He was only looking. Harold knew better than to buy this excuse. He knew that if people could come up with a reason, they could proceed with *any* act.

The Mackenzie on Insta didn't look exactly like the one on the lawn sign, and it took Harold a few minutes to realize why. The face, a tad plumper, was basically exact. But it was something else that Harold couldn't pinpoint until he reached picture number four. The round belly. The caption: "Entering the second trimester! Pray for me, ya'all."

To say Harold was taken aback by this reveal would be an understatement. He shoved the phone away and stood up. He opened the back porch door to get fresh air. After he collected himself, he snagged the bottle of bourbon and a 2-liter of ginger ale. Instead of his previous method for making a mixed drink, Harold took turns taking big swigs out of each bottle.

This must have done the trick because Harold woke up three hours later in the laundry room. He sat up and noticed that he had barfed on his chest. This alarmed him. People were known to die from choking on their vomit. That was the end of Harold's relationship with booze.

Harold crawled into bed with the guilt of a longtime drunk. He swore that he would behave better, starting in the morning. He would begin a brand-new chapter where physical and mental—primarily mental—health was paramount.

In the morning, Harold reviewed his "I never" list.

-I never married.

-I never had sex.

-I never had a date of any kind.

~~-I never had alcohol.~~

-I never did drugs.

~~-I never left the state.~~

-I never got a promotion.

-I never got a new car.

-I never fixed a car.

~~-I never had my own place.~~

~~-I never exercised (except when I was a kid in P.E. class).~~

~~-I never went to the doctor (after being checked out by grumpy nurses in schools).~~

~~-I never went on a diet.~~

-I never used a weapon.

-I never committed a crime.

Harold crossed off six out of fifteen in record time. He knew some could question his elimination of diet, but he was in the process of taking care of that. He opened the freezer and threw out two boxes of Jimmy Dean sandwiches. As a replacement, he had one of his mother's leftover Activia yogurts and a banana that was getting so dark it seemed like the only way to save it would be to include it in a bread.

Harold examined the rest of the list. The ones left to accomplish would require a level of patience he wasn't cut out for. Harold made the list shorter by tearing off the bottom of the page. He had no interest in using any sort of weapon, and he had no desire to commit a crime.

Harold got ready to walk for the second day in a row, but there was only one thing preventing him from getting a move on: his cell phone. He couldn't find it and had no recall of where he left it. The time or texting aspects were not important to him; tracking his time and calorie loss, on the other hand, was.

He took the same route as yesterday. As he neared the high school, he spotted a woman in the distance, a leggy blonde in head-to-toe spandex, removing yard signs from the grass. He accelerated to a pace he wasn't yet equipped to handle, and he paid for it. He had to pause to take a long breather. In the time he collected himself, the woman removed eleven signs. Despite his body begging him no, he pressed on.

He kept his head down as he passed the woman. She wasn't friendly anyway. She would accurately be labeled a "Karen" by nearly everyone she encountered. When Harold turned his head back to see what letter she was at, she barked at him with a gush of fury and vitriol.

"Are you checking out my ass?!"

"No, no, no. I am sorry."

"Yeah, yeah, yeah."

Harold swore she called him a "disgusting blob" under her breath. Once she departed from his view, he turned back. He had no interest in a walk, and it became all too clear to him why he had come outside today.

He was a danger to society, and he didn't like it. That "Karen" saved him from himself.

When he arrived home, he found his cell phone in the kitchen between a sugar jar and two empty soda bottles. How it got there didn't matter. He entered his pin and, to no surprise, had no texts or calls. He clicked on the Instagram icon with the sole intent of finally removing his mother's page from existence. But it did not open to his page or his mother's or even Mackenzie Welton's page.

It opened to one that belonged to Henna Gillespie. Shame filled Harold's body, and while he wanted—all he wanted—was to close out the app and continue a positive trajectory of checking items off his life's to-do list, he kept it open.

Image 1: Henna in a Salem State Sweatshirt. A poster with the word "Accepted!" hung near the back door.

Image 2: Henna bending down, cleavage loud and proud, in front of a "Happy 18th" cake.

Image 3: Henna wrapped in a towel at the beach with what appeared to be her mother.

Image 4: Henna not wrapped in a towel with a bikini top that was struggling to hold up what the Lord gave her.

Image 5: Henna sitting in a café. Name of establishment unknown.

Image 6: Henna in the same café serving an elderly customer a drink. Name of establishment on the back wall.

Image 7: Henna in a Daisy Duke outfit with a purple lollipop in her mouth.

It was here when Harold turned off his phone. He walked around aimlessly, unsure of what to do. He worked himself up so much that he put his phone in the freezer.

Harold went straight to bed, this time in his mother's room. But he realized that he forgot to clean her room as he promised himself the night before. He went straight to his room, crawled into bed, and tried to sleep. Every time he whispered, "Forget Henna," a stronger voice inside his head suggested he "Find Henna."

On the off chance that she would be at the café seen in pictures, Harold ventured out on foot. It took him seventeen minutes to make the journey. While he was somewhat concerned about building up a sweat, he knew that this was a reconnaissance mission and nothing more. He would sit outside at one of the tables and wait. Either she would show up as a worker or a customer. He thought the likelihood was high since cafes had just resumed their regular operating schedule.

Harold shifted in place in the metal chair that was too small for him. He had been here an hour, and only three customers had entered. *Slow day*, he thought. There was one positive. Henna was not inside working. This put him in a prime location to see all the comers and goers. Part of him worried that he would be there all day. As if he were speaking of the Devil, a VW bug pulled into the lot and then backed into a parking space right near the entrance. The driver's side door opened. A teenage girl with reddish-brown hair stood up, fixed the falling strap on her white cami top, and began walking towards the entrance.

Harold could not believe his luck. It was her!

Like his failure to control the voice that ordered him to find her, he was motivated by a new voice persuading him to get the heck out of there. Without looking in her direction, he sprung out of the chair. He hid in a hunting and sporting goods store.

After gasbagging with a few of her coworkers, Henna discarded the foam container that held her Chai Tea Latte in the recycle bin. She waved bye without words, lowered the Ray-Bans from her hair to eyes, and then made a beeline for the car she just inherited from her mother as a congratulatory gift for earning a full ride to the local university.

She unlocked the car from about one-hundred feet away. She could hear her mother moaning now.

"You should always unlock it right when you get to the vehicle. Lots of creepers out there. You never know."

Henna found her mother's overprotective nature exhausting and would frequently find ways to test the advice she received.

Henna grabbed the door handle, blew a hair out of her lip, and plopped down into the driver's seat. The second she did, a hand wrapped around her mouth. She bit the man's hand and screamed.

"Bite or scream again, and I'll have to use this."

Henna's eyes grew wide as a shiny blade moved towards her right cheek.

Harold could not believe he was acting in this manner. *Why did he purchase this knife? What purpose would it serve? Why was he threatening a young and attractive woman?*

He removed the bits about weapons and crime on his "I never" list. So, how did he land in this predicament?

"What do you want from me?" the girl pleaded.

"Drive."

"Where?"

"I don't know."

"You don't know?!"

"Where do you want to go?"

"Nowhere with you."

"I love you."

"You l-l-l-ove me?"

"I do. Love me back, or I'll hurt you."

Harold didn't mean it. He didn't know how the words left his lips. Perhaps it was the inner voices again. As Harold took a brief moment to ponder his verbal threat, Henna wrestled the knife away from him and jammed it into his neck.

Blood spurt into her hair, mask, and eyes. She abandoned the vehicle. Like the final girl in a horror film, Henna collapsed onto the pavement before regaining her balance. She ran towards the café without looking back.

Inside the VW bug, Harold Roberts bled to death. Before he did so, he praised Henna for being more beautiful in person. She was around to hear this compliment.

Harold's speech turned to incoherent mumbles. Harold thought about how those lawn signs—with first and last names provided—made it easy to stalk a person. Too easy. But all this was his fault. He knew that.

He had a vision of his mother. She was young and without Alzheimer's. It made him tear up.

"I'm sorry, Ma. I tried to find a life companion. I did. I really did."

But this desperate plea to his deceased mother in the final seconds of his life proved to be fruitless. His recent actions only assured the thing he feared most: dying alone.

ADAM VERSUS SUTTON

TERRY DENNIS WAITED outside a yellow colonial that, according to a red oval sign, was built in 1703. The place was haunted already; perhaps it had been so from its creation. He disliked moments of silence, so he occupied his mind by kicking the dead plants next to the patio.

Adam arrived earlier than the agreed-upon time. Regardless, Terry's body language conveyed that he was still somehow late. Adam pulled up in front of the home and put the truck in park; Sutton wanted to point out how far he was from the curb, but she focused all of her hateful energy on Terry.

"No."

"No, what?" Adam asked.

"You said you'd never meet with him again."

"I never said never."

"I'll stay here."

"Don't get out, and I'll drive right back to Connecticut."

"Fine by me."

For effect, Adam started up the vehicle. Usually, a major pushover, Sutton was surprised her dad was holding firm. *What had gotten into him?* She could see in his eyes that he meant business.

"He dresses like one of my classmates."

"A classmate you like?"

"A classmate I don't."

Adam took the time to size up his old friend. Sutton's fashion analysis was accurate. Terry sported red Converse All-Stars, plaid pants, and an orange tee with Leatherface on it. Behind the chainsaw-wielding legend, it said DISCO. If the term *boy-man* were listed in the dictionary, Terry's face would be plastered there right alongside it. Sutton had never seen the movie referenced on his tee, and she had no intention of doing so now. Whatever Terry liked, Sutton committed to hating. Forever.

Adam turned the truck off. Sutton opened the door, stepped out, and slammed the door for effect. Unlike most folks in Sutton's path, Terry was not the slightest bit intimidated by her.

"Happy as ever, I see."

"Shut your mouth," Sutton barked.

"Somebody's a high schooler."

Terry cracked up at his remark. Adam approached and put his hand out. Terry stared at it. They locked eyes.

"A handshake for a pal since fourth grade?! No, no, NO. We hug, pal."

Terry pulled Adam in for a bear hug.

"Are you pals?" Sutton dared to ask.

"For life," Terry said with pride.

"Is that why you stole his company?"

"Sut," Adam warned.

Sutton glared at her father for chiming in with the name abbreviation. Terry smirked in a manner that suggested he was holding back a slew of comebacks for the snarky teen.

"Did I steal? Is that what you told her, old buddy?"

"I told her no such thing," Adam said.

"Girl needs to review her facts."

"Don't call me girl."

"Should I call you boy? Or woman? You're neither."

"Don't call me anything."

"I won't call you anything. Just don't call me a thief."

The trip was already a disaster. If Adam didn't intervene and end this spat between his child and the man-child, he could risk making Sutton's situation worse.

"Guys!"

"I'm not a guy, Dad! Jesus H!"

"The fighting needs to stop," Adam pleaded.

Terry and Sutton went silent. Adam succeeded as a moderator. He could get down to business and see if what was inside the home could provide a mental cure to his daughter's frequent and mysterious woes.

But then Terry whispered a comeback under his breath. And Sutton engaged for battle yet again.

"Can you just admit that you stole his show?!" Sutton shouted.

"Can you just admit that you have no idea what you're bleeping talking about?"

Adam gave Terry a look. He puts his hands up in defense.

"I said bleeping."

"My father should sue you for all you're worth."

Terry guffawed at Sutton's preposterous idea. Adam was baffled about why his daughter cared so much about Terry's newfound success on television. Sure, Adam and Terry were the stars of a public-access TV show called The North Shore Ghosters from 2006 until 2008. They were both credited with the lead investigator title, and their differing styles (mainly personalities) made for a good distraction if you were into the ghost thing. Each episode, of which there were only a handful (the burden of a low budget), revolved around Adam and Terry investigating a home where paranormal activity was raging. There weren't many interesting cases—save one at their present location—that commanded the nearby communities' interest. The case scarred Adam for life, and it spooked Terry into reconsidering his only career plan.

"Sue for what? Willingly relinquishing his rights to me?" Terry asked.

"He didn't do that willingly."

"Yes, I did," Adam chimed in.

Sutton went silent. Adam knew this wasn't the kind of silence she reserved for people she didn't want to talk to; this was the kind of silence that served as a momentary reboot before she launched into another verbal attack.

"Why on earth would you do that?!"

"He had his reasons," Terry offered.

Sutton shot Terry a look as if to say, "Not talking to you, dude." What she didn't understand and what she, apparently sooner rather than later, would discover is that Terry, for all his bravado, wasn't to blame for anything. Adam left the show. *He* relocated back to his parents' home in Connecticut to grieve. *He* ignored all of Terry's incoming calls, texts, and email messages for half a decade. *He* sold his portion (50%) of the show rights because he wanted nothing to do with the paranormal world anymore. *He* needed to erase that part of his past and get a job—any job—that would provide him with enough money to care for his going-on-five-years-of-age daughter. Terry hadn't tricked him.

Terry wasn't a wolf in sheep's clothing. Terry was a man who believed that the show could transfer to regular TV and, if marketed correctly, would reach a niche audience. Terry was right all along. Once he met a pair of twin investors with deep pockets from Brooklyn, the days of bad camerawork and bad lighting were gone. He revamped *Ghosters* into *Paranormal Patrol*. Terry deserved a few eyebrow-raises for casting two beautiful women as his assistant and researcher, but his dogged determination is what won the game here and it was the reason, more than the investors' financial backing, that his show became a national success. And he always wanted Adam to stay on the ride—he did absolutely everything he could—but he fully understood why his friend got off when he did.

"Name one reason, Terry."

Terry licked his lips and smiled big and wide. Adam knew there was no stopping Terry now.

"Your. Mother."

Adam felt guilty for allowing Terry to reveal the main issue here. Ever since childhood, he preferred it when someone would say the things he needed to get off his chest. Him and conflict didn't mix.

"She died in a car accident when I was 4. I do not see the connection."

Terry exchanged a look with Adam. He wondered how far he should proceed. This wasn't his information to share.

"The man wasn't allowed to grieve?"

"Of course, he was. But your show made a comeback last year."

"Meaning?"

"Why isn't he involved? Why isn't he rich and famous like you?"

"Because he doesn't want to be!"

"You're such a traitor."

"Hey!"

Adam couldn't take it anymore. It's one thing if Sutton were correct in her attacks, but she, as it stood, was already wrong on two accounts.

"He is not a thief, and he is no traitor," Adam continued.

"Stand up for yourself, Dad. God! Stop being such a pathetic loser and stand up to him! God, I wish it was you instead of her."

Sutton had been cold to him lately. She barely looked at him. She rarely, if ever, spoke to him. She even failed to acknowledge his recent birthday. But all of that added up paled into comparison with being called a pathetic loser by the child you have done everything for. Not to mention, her wishing that he had perished instead of his wife.

Tears formed in Adam's eyes. Terry made a move to reach for him. Adam shook his head and walked off in no particular direction. Sutton watched him go; Terry studied her until Adam vanished around a street corner.

"You proud of yourself? Feel like you, uh, accomplished something here at this particular moment?"

"Shut up, dude."

"You shut up," Terry fired back.

Sutton snorted, mumbled what sounded like a swear under her breath, and headed towards the truck. Terry, unable to control himself even though he knew he should, delivered the last words:

"You got that tiny head so far up your behind that you'll never comprehend what that man has done for you."

Sutton reached the truck, opened the passenger door, hopped inside, and slammed it even harder than she did upon arrival.

REVENGE TOUR

EDWARD SHIFTED his butt because the wax paper was driving him crazy. The action didn't help, so he crumpled it up and tossed it across the room. He was tired of waiting. This is why he hated medical offices. There was no way to indicate whether they would give you good or bad news because they made everyone wait. You had to wait in the lobby long after your assigned time, you had to wait for a nurse, you had to wait for a doctor, you had to wait for the results of whatever the doctor had tested, and you had to wait if they wanted to take a second look at something.

This is where Edward found himself. If the doctor's office wanted to bill him for the wax paper, he would accept it.

The doctor, a man of significant height and insignificant weight, entered the room with a facemask. He noticed the missing wax paper straight away, glanced towards the corner, back at Edward, and then smirked. He dragged a stool across the floor in a manner that seemed pompous. He parked it at the edge of the bed and then placed his hairy hand on Edward's kneecap. Even though the doctor had gloves on, Edward didn't like the gesture.

"No way to say it, kiddo. You have it. The virus."

The virus seemed so abstract a few weeks back. It started in Thailand and traveled in quick succession to Italy, England, France, and then Canada. The politicians in the United States promised that it would never get here; the medical professionals guaranteed it would.

Edward turned beet red at the doctor's news. He thought this would be written off as the typical cold based on the common symptoms that were, with or without medication, relatively easy to handle.

"What do I do?" Edward asked.

"Pray," the doctor joked.

Edward wanted to slap him across the face. The doctor stopped snickering.

"Your symptoms aren't as bad as they could be, but that's what's so difficult about this virus: For you, it might feel like a regular cold. For, say, your grandma, it could feel like death."

"It could kill her?'

"It could."

"I could kill my grandma?"

"Please don't."

"Obviously. But I, what I have, can kill her?"

"You need to quarantine for at least fourteen days. Bare minimum! Keep your distance from her. Make sure she keeps her distance from you."

"Where am I gonna freaking sleep? The basement?"

"That or the attic."

"There's a storm door that leads to the basement."

"Oh, perfect. Use that."

"The school gonna understand why I'm taking two weeks off or—"

"They don't want you anywhere near their building. Trust me. The school might even shut down because of you."

Edward left the doctor's office in a mental fog. He couldn't believe he had caught *the virus*. He feared germs. At school, he often yelled at his peers for not washing their hands post-bathroom or coughing into their hands without giving it a second thought. They called him a freak; he called them poster children for abortion.

When Edward arrived home, he did not enter through the storm door that leads to the basement. He walked straight through the front door, passed through the living room, hugged and kissed his knitting grandma, and then made his way toward his bedroom.

"Hold it, Buster."

Edward stopped in his tracks. He feared that his grandmother already knew his diagnosis. Since it was *the virus*, it wasn't unreasonable to think that the doctor placed a call to her to keep her in the loop. Her life, after all, was at stake.

"Forget something?"

He stared at her. He was unsure what she was driving at.

"I'm fine. Typical cold symptoms. The doc wants me to get something, um, called Mucinex."

Mucinex was the first brand that came to his brain. His grandmother's expression remained the same. She wasn't curious about his doctor's visit at all. Perhaps she had forgotten that he even had an appointment. He followed her eyes as they shifted towards his feet.

"So sorry."

Edward removed his boots and carried them to the hall closet that was adjacent to the front door.

"Have a crap-ton of homework to do!" shouted Edward as he hurried towards his bedroom.

Edward shut his bedroom door and closed his eyes. *That was close*, he thought. He was sure she would know what was wrong with him. He plopped onto his lime green beanbag chair and stared at the ceiling. He, a goddamn teenager, had *the virus*. But how? Wasn't the disease strictly targeting the elderly and those with compromised immune systems?

Edward took out his cell phone. For no more than a few seconds, he considered calling Salem High to inform them of his positive results. He knew that that was the decent and humane approach; however, he opted for something a bit more sinister.

He took a deep breath and reflected on his high school existence. He had no friends or girlfriends. He had no acquaintances. He would have considered himself a ghost had he not been picked on by jocks, cheerleaders, and occasional teachers throughout his three-year tenure at Salem High.

Instead of being a responsible being, instead of being a decent human, Edward would, after lengthy contemplation, quietly spread the disease that everyone in his country had become terrified of.

His first target was Everett McGill. The sole reason Everett earned a place at the summit was for the mere fact that he'd bullied Edward ever since they were in the third grade.

Edward arrived at school an hour early because Everett, athlete galore, met one of his teachers for daily tutoring before any of his classes started.

Edward paused in front of Everett's locker. No one was around. Not even a janitor. He spat on the locker and smeared the phlegmy contents all over the door handle.

Even though Edward could rank her number one on the list, Olivia Woods was next. She earned the second-place position due to her frequent taunts of Edward. He had never done anything to her. He had, at least according to his standpoint, ignored her completely. She was fascinated with him, however, and not in a good way. Whenever she would pass by him in the halls, she would cough and, under her breath, say, "Caterpillar!" She would laugh, and her friends, a group of high-pitched blondes, would join her. The tone of the laughs always enraged Edward, but he never said or did anything about it.

Today was different. Motivated by the stunt he'd pulled at Everett's locker, he aimed to elevate his revenge game.

After the homeroom bell rang, Edward made his way into the halls, into a blended sea of ninth thru twelfth graders. Olivia wasn't hard to locate. She was, like every morning of her high school life, hanging out in the mall (or lobby area) with her friends. Olivia flirted with Mr. Banks, the track coach. Edward knew very little about relationships, but he would bet his life on the fact that Olivia and the adult would, if they hadn't already, engage in sexual relations. Olivia always waited until the second bell—the get your butt to class, or you'll get written up bell—before heading to her first class.

The second the bell rang, Edward made a break for Olivia's direction. Simultaneously, she proceeded towards the Art wing. In a manner that would impress Buster Keaton, Edward stumbled over his feet and crashed, head-on, with Olivia. She fell backward and took two of her nameless and voiceless blondes with her.

Olivia flipped out. She tried to spring her body upwards, but Edward kept his upper body above her lower half. She delivered a deluge of insults his way, catching the attention of the nearby security guard. After she called him "a piece of poor white trash," she turned her attack back to Edward.

"Shave that eyebrow! You're supposed to have two of them!"

Edward smiled. Her rage lessened out of confusion. He coughed into her face once, twice, and a third time for good measure. She slapped him. He took it without incident. He stood up and motioned for her to pass by; she ran in the direction of her first-period class. Her cronies lagged.

"Leave, or I'll cough on you, too."

The cronies screamed bloody murder. Like chickens released from a cage, they ran off in random directions, completely forgetting the location of their next class. The security guard sized up Edward.

"Am I in trouble?"

"No."

"Then I won't infect you."

"Thank you."

Aside from the security guard, Edward felt next to nothing for everyone inside that building. This is why he continued his germ-spreading rampage. He walked down every single hallway wing (named after the primary colors) and dragged his contaminated hands across every locker, every door handle, and every surface that he could.

A month later, the school was closed indefinitely. They shifted to distance learning after a high number of students and staffers tested positive for the virus. Everett was sick for ten days straight. While he recovered, Edward took great solace in the fact that his actions had canceled the fall and winter sports. Olivia, target number two, wasn't so lucky. She suffered through a seven-day hospital stint where she went in and out of a comatose state. She was never the same.

Edward's grandmother died inside the home. She started with common cold symptoms and then graduated to bouts of panic and breathlessness. She pleaded with Edward to take her to the hospital because she had "a lot more living and drinking to do!" He ignored every plea by cranking up the volume on his video games. She stopped breathing in her rocking chair; she left this world thinking that the Thai people took her life away when it was, in fact, the one she promised to take care of after her son and his wife died in a freak plane accident. It was her very own blood.

UNDER SURVEILLANCE

MY OWNERS, a male couple with a gargantuan age gap between them, have reached a breaking point in their relationship. Only one of them is aware of it, however.

The innocent one is a devoted elementary Art teacher. He amuses me to no end with his random choices of hair color (pink and purple now) and Disney-related outfits. Even though I have never had the privilege of seeing him teach a class because, well, cats aren't allowed in schools, I believe that he must be worth whatever salary the district dishes out. I hear him talk about the kids all the time. He doesn't do it in a perverted way, either. He truly cares about them.

The guilty one is the manager of a trendy cafe down the road. He is moody all the time. Nothing makes him happy. For example, he received a positive write-up in the press recently, which credited his establishment with the Best Brunch on the North Shore! Instead of being pleased with such praise, he asked how he could become the Best Brunch in the entire state. The one thing he has going for him, which pains me to admit is that he is devilishly handsome. He rocks the salt and pepper hair combo like a professional. He could work the desk of a news network instead of sweating over customers' breakfast needs.

While their relationship started off with quality communication and lots of intimacy (gag alert), it has, at the three-year mark, crash-landed into something resembling a roommate situation.

The innocent one lives in denial. He tries to make it work. He still sends flowers to the guilty one's workplace. He always surprises him with gifts. He even cleans the apartment and does all of their laundry. And why does he do this? He wants the ring.

The ring, of which there is none, is the carrot that the innocent one will chase until the end of time. But I know that the guilty one has no plans or interest in ever purchasing one. How do I know this? Because the guilty one makes comments under his breath—I have excellent hearing—that speaks to the contrary. If he dares to voice his opinion out loud, he will playfully question the innocent one in this manner: "Think you deserve one?"

The guilty one has all the leverage, and he exploits it for all its worth. That system is about to end, though. Despite the innocent one being oblivious to the rampant infidelity, I have become aware of it. The leverage is all mine now.

One should always be kind to cats because they see all. The innocent one has not only been a saint in the relationship and at his workplace, but he has been incredibly kind to me. He rubs my head, chin, and the favorite spot above my tail without me prompting him to do so. He provides me with treats, cat crunch, and a variety of canned food that would make any cat jealous.

Whenever it is just the two of us, the guilty one goes out of his way to harass me. He shoos me away for no reason. He calls me stupid. He claims that I have dandruff. He teases me and with great pride and says things like, "We have plenty of cans, and you're not getting one" or "Take a bath, and maybe you'll get a treat, fatty." I don't appreciate the harassment one bit. It hurts my feelings. But nothing hurts as much as witnessing a good man, the innocent one, put his heart and soul into a relationship that is worth next to nothing.

Believe you me, I have tried to expose the guilty one on multiple occasions. I located his alternate cellular phone and nudged it out into the open for the innocent one to discover during a vacuuming session. The guilty one found it at the last second.

I pried a receipt out of the trash receptacle. At a glance, the crumpled paper proved that the guilty one had too many martinis that late September afternoon. If one studied it scrupulously, one would follow the line from the bartender's name (Otto) to the arrow at the bottom right-hand corner of the paper. The message on the back made me ill. It read, "Call me ASAP, handsome." I batted this paper around and chased it through the apartment's interior. All I wanted was for the innocent one to pick it up, open it, and read it. I meowed endlessly. Confused, the innocent one gave me treats. I refused to eat them to make my point land. The innocent one tossed the paper into the trash again.

This brings me to my latest attempt to catch the guilty one in his tracks. Later this morning, Otto, the one made famous by the receipt, intends to visit for a little bedroom rendezvous (gag alert again). No infidelity has ever occurred inside this apartment, so pardon my announced distaste for such an event. The innocent one, of course, will be at work. I have thought long and hard about getting the innocent one to witness the infidelity. But I don't know how to use a cell phone. They used to be easier to understand. Now, most of them have unique technology, which requires a face or handprint. I doubt either of my paws would allow me to sign-in to the guilty one's device. Otherwise, I would tape the whole act and send it as one of those text message thingies to the innocent one. This would break his heart for sure, but he would become privy to the truth, and he would be able to move on, with me, in this apartment or a better one that didn't symbolize a land of cheating.

My plan, of which I am confident will breed success, ignores the guilty party altogether and focuses, with all its might, on the compassionate nature of the innocent party. Love him as much as I do, he is the weak link in the chain. Therefore, I must exploit him once for the greater good.

Mere minutes before he is to depart for work—he is busy in the bathroom—I will deliver a performance that an audience, specifically a paid one, would be in awe of.

The innocent one vacates the bathroom and makes a pit stop in the kitchen. He turns on the machine that spits out hot black liquid, or Keurig as he calls it. He rubs his eyes and stretches; he is still trying to wake up. While his mental guard might be down, I know what will make him come to life. He doesn't need the black liquid for what he is about to witness.

I meow. He doesn't look! He always looks when I meow. I put together a succession of meows that would make one think I was an aspiring composer. He looks my way, and I, momentarily caught in the moment, almost roll over and purr. Luckily I don't, because this would defeat the point and value of my upcoming performance.

The innocent one returns his attention to the hot liquid as it hisses to announce its completion. He squirts a dollop of honey into his cup and pours half and half—the liquid that makes all felines swoon—into his "Life Isn't Art" mug. He goes for his first sip. This is when I begin the performance.

I stretch my eyes out like a bug and start to gag. He turns my way. I have his attention now, and I intend to keep it. It hurts to be sick; it hurts more to pretend you're sick. Still, this is worth it if I achieve my desired results.

"You okay, sweetie?"

Yes, I am perfectly fine; however, I am making myself retch for your future benefit. This is how much I love you. I don't have to say any of this because cats cannot produce unnecessary dialogue that humans do.

I vomit bits of crunch onto the carpet. He puts his coffee mug down and approaches. He bends down and rubs my head. I give him the "I might be dying" look, and I can tell, by his eyebrows sudden dip downwards, that he is officially concerned.

"Got a tummy ache?"

I force more crunch out of my system. Even I am surprised by the amount that comes out. I lie on my side and, risky as it may be, wheeze like I am mere hours away from death's door.

He rushes into the bedroom. I hear him waking the guilty one. If nothing else, I am happy to disturb the cheater's sleep. I extend my claws and pull my body a few inches forward. I need to hear all of their dialogue.

The guilty one, no surprise whatsoever, is yelling at his innocent partner. I don't care for his limited vocabulary; it consists mostly of profanities anyway.

The innocent one returns to my area and sits on the floor with me. I snap out of a mode of curiosity and switch to one of pain and suffering. It bothers him to see me in this state. The greater good is at stake, so this is no time whatsoever for a guilty conscience. The show, as they say, must go on.

"I have to go to work, bud."

No, no, no. I want to scream, but all I have are meows at my disposal. I crank them up for all their worth and rise to a crescendo of barf. It brings tears to his eyes. He rushes to the kitchen to snag paper towels. While he cleans, he tells me that I am going to be okay. I know

I am okay, but I need to convince him that I will never be the same again. He pets the top of my head and rubs my chin. He promises to call the vet (doctor for animals), think about me all day, and snuggle with me the second he returns. I watch him leave and realize that my efforts, my epic performance, was all for naught.

Minutes later, the guilty one exits the bedroom and checks on my condition. He snorts. I don't know what to make of this sound until he follows it with these remarks:

"Aw, looks like the fatty overate again. Stupid cat. I wish you would croak."

The guilty one heads into the bathroom and abandons me. I like being away from him for obvious reasons, but I need a new plan or something to go my way. At this current moment, my plan is an unmitigated disaster.

While the guilty one showers, his cellular buzzes. I hop onto the marble countertop and peek at the text message. It is from Otto. He says he will be here around 12:30. I check the clock. Math is a tricky area for me; however, I am reasonably sure that this man—and instant rival of the innocent one—should arrive in less than three hours.

The hours feel like years. And yet, I cannot for the life of me dream up another idea to take the guilty one down. Someone knocks at the door. I panic. Not only have I not generated a backup plan, but I am, more likely than not, going to have to listen to the two engage in a vigorous bout of lovemaking. *Oh, dear me! I am out of time. I am nothing but a failure!*

The guilty one lets in this Otto fellow. Despite my best efforts to be objective, I cannot see what the attraction is. The innocent one is much more handsome!

They start kissing. I want to vomit for real at this point. It is too much for me to handle. If either one of them leaves the front door or a window open, I will run off. I deserve to become a stray for failing the innocent one in this manner.

The guilty one leads Otto down the hallway and shoves him into the bedroom. The door slams. Moments later, the moaning is underway. I close my eyes, hoping against hope that I will never wake up. That is about the only solution to my problem.

Then, as if God himself had returned to this apartment to deliver me positive news, the front door opened. And, lucky day, the innocent one appeared.

"You okay, sweetheart? I took a half-day just for you. We're going to the vet, okay? We're going to fix whatever's going on in that tummy-tum."

His eyes drift away from me. He glances in the direction of the bedroom. He marches down the hallway and bursts through the bedroom door. Men scream. Men argue. Otto flees the apartment with nothing on but his boxer shorts. The guilty one pleads with the innocent one. Finally, for the only time that I have witnessed, there is a reverse of power in this relationship. The innocent one kicks the guilty one out of the apartment and informs him that they, as of this day, are over.

I roll over on my back and stare at the ceiling. The innocent one approaches.

"You feeling better?"

Much, I would love to say. *I am feeling much, much better.*

PRESSURE COOKER

THE BRIDE-TO-BE HAD DREAMED of her wedding day since the time she was six.

Yet here she was in a hotel bathroom, filled with what she would define as dread. Her mother, oblivious to her current mental woes, applied the headpiece. Where did these thoughts come from? Why were they occurring now?

The bride-to-be had the occasional panic attack, but a gum-chewing session or a lengthy bout of rest buried under the comforter usually provided the cure. This feeling was different. It wasn't a panic attack at all; it was a panic explosion.

"You ready? Your Prince Charming is waiting," her mother said.

Her husband-to-be was no prince. He was, however, a man with a quality job (guidance counselor), a man with a nice home (saltbox colonial), a man with great credit (score of 735), and a man with a credible personality (respectful and honest). There was nothing wrong with him. If pushed to find something, the bride-to-be would clutch at straws and then eventually concede that he possessed two behavioral ticks that drove her up the wall: he always left the cap off the toothpaste, and he ate the skins on his potatoes.

Any wife would be thrilled to put up with such quirks so long as their man—if they married a man—had a quality job (guidance counselor), a nice home (saltbox colonial), a great credit score (735), and a credible personality (respectful and honest).

The bride-to-be screamed inside. Her mother, still oblivious, sized her up with pride.

"Most beautiful bride I have seen."

"Thanks, Mom."

"Everyone's on the roof. You ready?"

"Mom?"

"Yes?"

"Nothing."

Most mothers would have detected something off at this particular moment. They would have stopped their daughter and asked something along the clichéd lines of "Is everything okay?" or "Are you doing all right?"

The bride-to-be's mother was like most mothers. Unfortunately, on her daughter's most important day of existence, she was three sheets to the damn wind. The hiccups proved it.

"Need anything before you head up there?"

The bride-to-be needed a hug. She needed someone to swear that it would all be okay. She needed someone to promise that she had the mental fortitude to tackle anything that came with the pressures of getting and staying married.

The bride-to-be followed her mother's lead down the L-shaped hallway that was decked out in Halloween decorations, avoided a moody cleaning woman and her excessive trash bin, and stopped in front of the elevator doors.

"Are you kidding me?"

A pink piece of construction paper hung from the elevator doors. It read, "Out of order." The bride-to-be figured this was a sign that her life, one with a perfectly decent man, was doomed. All the signs said so.

"They gonna make us take the f—"

"Mom, don't swear. It stresses me out."

"It stresses me out, too. But it's four goddamn flights to the rooftop."

The bride-to-be and her mother waited for any employee to return to the front desk area. No one came. The mother's cell phone burst to life and at maximum volume.

"Hello?!"

The bride-to-be watched her mother try to get a word in edge-wise. But the bride-to-be's father wasn't having it.

"Christ almighty, that man didn't give me a chance to freaking explain."

"I need to sit down."

"Sit? Your dad'll freak. James'll wonder if you're even going to marry him. We've got to go."

The bride-to-be complied with her mother's demand and, after sizing up the vacant front desk area one last time, ascended the nearby marble staircase.

"If your father calls me again, I swear on God's green earth that I will snap."

"Stay calm, please."

"I am calm. I will stay calm. As long as he doesn't call me again. Can't even let me explain what was wrong with the elevator. Can't even let me explain why we're running late. What kind of person doesn't let you explain?"

"Mom, stop talking."

The bride-to-be's mother kept bitching; however, she decreased her volume. They made it to the third floor without much complaint.

"Why were there no front desk people?"

The bride-to-be wanted to muzzle her mother. She would have emptied her savings account for a roll of duct tape so she could wrap it around the drunk woman's mouth.

"This is like hiking Mt. Washington."

The bride-to-be glared at her mother. Perhaps tape wouldn't suffice; a sharp object or bottle of arsenic would get the job done.

"How are you doing? Y'okay?"

"Do I look okay?"

The bride-to-be sweated profusely. Wet rings formed around her armpits, and her makeup, which had taken nearly an hour to apply, was ruined. She didn't need a mirror to prove it.

"You look...fine."

"*Fine* on my wedding day?"

"I don't know who they got running this place. Nobody at the front desk. Gotta climb a mountain to have a wedding. This is—"

"Let's keep going. I'll fix my face up there."

"If your father bugs us again, I swear—"

Before the bride-to-be got the chance to object to her mother's position on the matter, the cell phone rang again.

"I'm not answering."

"Good choice, Mom."

"But if he calls again after me not answering, I am going to—"

"One more floor."

"This hotel owes us a discount. Should comp the entire ceremony for this crap. Feel like I've run a marathon. And I'm in shape. Aren't I in shape?"

The bride-to-be nodded. She refused to respond since it just kept her mother rambling.

Her mother's phone rang again. She answered.

"Stop yelling! We'll be there in thirty seconds. We could turn around and leave the hotel if you'd prefer that. Would you prefer that?!"

This response silenced the father. The bride-to-be's mother ended the call and shook her head.

"Why did I marry him?"

The bride-to-be noticed the door that led to the roof. She was less than sixty feet away from the destination she craved since childhood.

"Would you do that, Mom?"

"Do what?"

Turn around and leave the hotel for me?

The bride-to-be never asked this question. Had she done so, it would have been too late anyway. Her mother's hand nudged the silver bar in the middle of the door. Sunlight invaded the stairwell and blinded the bride-to-be.

She walked fifty feet before turning the corner. White roses lined the ground. Her husband-to-be locked eyes with her. It was evident to her that he was excited about this ceremony.

The bride-to-be's mother whispered in her father's ear, "What the hell is wrong with you? Can't let me explain what happened?"

The father, wearing a mismatched blazer and pants, laughed it off. "You trying to ruin her wedding? I'm not trying to ruin her wedding."

"Guys, please."

Mother and father ended their bickering. The mother took a seat in front and checked out, in a sexual manner, her future son-in-law and the Justice of the Peace. The bride-to-be took her father's calloused hand (results of a lifelong career as a construction worker worker) and walked down the makeshift aisle. Classical music, cued up by the unseen wedding planner, played in the background.

The husband-to-be perked up a bit, remarked under his breath how beautiful his bride-to-be was, and then waited as she was led towards him by her father. The Justice of the Peace tapped the husband-to-be's back—a choreographed gesture to remind him to retrieve his bride-to-be.

The bride-to-be squeezed the bouquet with all her might; she clung to it like it was her lifesaver. Right as the handoff from father to husband-to-be occurred, the bride-to-be tossed the bouquet behind her, veered off at a diagonal to the right, and leaped off the roof.

The father screamed. The mother covered her face. The husband-not-to-be fainted. The other guests remained frozen in their seats. The Justice of the Peace strolled towards the edge of the roof and glimpsed down at the cobblestone Salem street. He didn't know that the young woman had dreamed of being a bride since the age of six.

REBECCA FROST

SUTTON HAD BEEN inside the truck for fourteen minutes. Her father, who ran off in a huff, hadn't returned. *Where would he even go in this strange city?*

Terry approached the truck and grabbed the passenger door handle. Locked.

"Open up," he ordered.

Sutton shook her head.

"Come out here and talk to me or let me inside."

Sutton took out her cell phone. No texts or calls. Totally unlike her father. He must be pissed.

"Gonna ignore me? Okay, ignore me."

Terry walked away. Sutton didn't follow him with her eyes. Instead, she checked Insta. She clicked on the arrow in the upper right-hand corner of her home page. She clicked on the message she had sent to Zoe Wilde. It said *Seen*. Sutton wanted to die a slow death. It was painful enough when Zoe hadn't viewed it. But now, knowing that it had been viewed by her crush made it feel like a new form of torture.

All of a sudden, the truck rocked up and down. She looked in the rearview mirror and saw Terry Dennis, her enemy, hopping up and down with a maniacal look on his face.

"I can do this all day! Let me inside the truck, so I can tell you why you should love your father more."

To take her mind off Zoe and to get the truck's movement to stop, Sutton hit the unlock button on her side. The driver's side door lock shot right up into the unlock position. Terry scooted off the bed and joined Sutton inside. There was an epic silence that even made Sutton, Queen of Not Talking, uncomfortable.

"Your mother didn't die in a car accident."

Sutton powered off her phone and gave Terry her undivided attention.

Meanwhile, at The Good Morning Café, Adam Frost sat in a green leather booth drinking his second cup of coffee. He studied the interior with all its black and white photos of the eatery's 75-year existence. The interior hadn't changed since he frequented the place a decade ago.

A middle-aged waitress with round hips and poofy hair approached.

"Y'make a decision yet, darling?"

"Shockingly enough, yes. I would like a cheddar cheese omelet with broccoli, hash browns, sourdough toast, and a single pancake. One of the huge ones."

"Flavor?"

"Chocolate chip."

The waitress scribbled on her pad and then took his gigantic menu. Adam stopped her before she walked away.

"One other thing: I've never had a drink-drink."

"You need to get out more."

"When I entered, one of the ladies was making a drink with orange juice and—"

"That's a mimosa."

"Can I try one?"

"Should I be worried if I get you one?"

"I'll be fine."

"If you trash the place, you're paying for it."

"Deal."

Adam needed this type of exchange. It didn't matter if he liked the morning cocktail. A cooler dad would order a drink; a pathetic loser would do the opposite. He needed to change his ways and embrace life more, even if it was in baby steps.

Back at the colonial, Sutton listened as Terry explained what happened to her mother.

"There are certain things your father should tell you, but he can't tell you this. He won't tell you this. He doesn't have the strength."

"What happened to my mother?"

"She had a CHD." Sutton's eyebrows narrowed. Terry continued. "Congenital heart defect. Since childhood."

"She had a heart attack?"

"More or less."

"I don't get why that would need to be a big secret."

"Ghost hunters and heart conditions don't exactly mix well. It's like you and me."

Ghost hunters and heart conditions? Sutton's brain processed what he was telling her.

"My mother was a ghost hunter?"

"Came up with the idea for our show."

"So, you stole the idea from her?"

"I DID NOT STEAL ANYTHING! YOUR FATHER SOLD ME THE RIGHTS!"

"You don't need to scream at me."

"YES, I DO!"

"Why?"

"Because you're a brat that's got it better than every single kid I've ever met."

"I have it better than—"

"Every single kid, yes."

"Why?"

Terry took a deep breath, exhaled, and then continued with the following:

"Because your daddy, whom you so rudely labeled *pathetic loser,* took the substantial sum of money he received for his portion of the show's rights and he dropped it, every single cent, into a trust for the pain in the ass faux-victim I'm currently chatting with."

Sutton was stunned. She couldn't process what she learned about her mother and she felt a tremendous pang of guilt for being so cruel to her father.

"Why would he keep that a secret?"

"Maybe 'cuz his daughter barely talks to him. Maybe 'cuz his daughter ignores him on his birthday."

Sutton couldn't believe it. She totally blanked. *How could she have forgotten his fortieth birthday?* In the past, she made a big deal about him getting older. *Ugh,* she thought. *What kind of child treats their parent this way?*

"I need to talk to him."

"And apologize."

"And talk. But how are we going to find him?"

"Call 911 and report a missing person."

"Seriously?"

"Definitely not. I know where he is."

"Why? He text you?"

"No." Sutton's eyes narrowed. "Your father's predictable."

As depressed as he was, Adam couldn't finish the mimosa. There were those that drank and those that didn't. He was relieved he didn't respond to the bubbly liquid in a positive manner. He shoved the last piece of chocolate chip pancake into his mouth. He stared off at nothing in particular, recalling how he and his wife used to visit this place weekly. He put his head down on the table.

"You okay?" a familiar voice asked.

Adam lifted his head. Sutton sat across from him. The tone of her question sounded like she was actually concerned about another human being for once.

"I am not."

"Why did Mom have a heart attack?"

"Why do you cut your arms?"

Sutton's face flushed at his question. She didn't know her dad was privy to her developing habit.

"I...don't...know."

"Then I don't know why your mother had a heart attack."

Sutton didn't appreciate her father playing hardball. It wasn't his natural style. But given his discovery about her, she couldn't exactly blame him for the hard-nosed approach.

"I'm not going to...off myself if that's what you're wondering."

"I didn't ask if you were going to do that. I asked why you cut your arms," Adam said sternly.

The waitress passed at this exact moment and instead of asking the young lady if she wanted to order anything, she kept moving towards a vacant booth in the corner.

"It's complicated. Can you, um, go first?"

Adam studied his daughter. Her hair, normally covering her eyes and nose, was brushed back. He could tell she was open to have a heart-to-heart. He always wondered how this moment would play out. Sure enough, it was occurring in Salem, the place that impacted his life journey more than any other.

"I didn't witness the event that took her life. But Terry has the audio of it somewhere. And *no*, you're not allowed to hear it. You're not old enough."

Sutton attempted to speak, but Adam put his finger up. She held her opinion back.

"Long story very short, a suburban family in this city was being tormented by what, according to many paranormal investigators, was a demonic force. Said force had its sights on the family's only child: a three-year-old boy. Well, your saint of a mother, God rest her soul, didn't like that very much. Despite promising Terry and me that she wouldn't assist with a required exorcism due to her heart condition, she tried to help anyway. The priest was so traumatized by the event that he left the parish. Your mother didn't survive."

"Were you mad at her?"

"I still am. Your turn."

Sutton locked eyes with her father. She almost informed him that a huge chocolate chip was on his right cheek, but she opted against it because it would ruin their first serious conversation.

"I have...a lot going on in my head."

"Such as...?"

"It's hard to explain. Feels like static, you know? Like I'm trying to find the right channel, but the right one isn't like, um, ever working." Adam appeared confused. "I don't know. I should prolly speak to a professional or something."

"But will you speak to a professional?"

"I'd tell them more than you."

"Promise to go and I'll stop asking."

"I...

"And promise to eat."

With conviction, Sutton made her promises. They hoofed it back to the truck where, to no one's surprise, Terry was sitting on the front stoop. He watched as Sutton shoved the rest of a bacon, egg, and cheese into her mouth.

"Thanks for getting me food," Terry said sarcastically.

"I can go back if you like," Adam offered.

Terry stood up and stretched. A big grin developed on his face.

"You need to go inside."

"We're pooped. Going to head back home. It's been a long day."

"You can't leave without going inside. This is why you brought her here!"

"It is?" Sutton wondered.

"It was," Adam said.

"She should go in there."

Adam turned to Sutton. She had no clue why this old home mattered. He didn't feel like telling her why it did and he didn't care to expose her, at fourteen years of age, to whatever paranormal activity was occurring inside.

"Sutton, be a doll and wait out here for a few," Terry said.

"Will do. But call me doll again and you'll pay the consequences."

Terry cracked up, put his arm around Adam's shoulder and guided him toward the house. Sutton got inside the truck and occupied her brain with her cell phone.

Adam made it four steps into the home before he paused. "I can't do this."

"The activity isn't down here."

"I. Can't. Be. In. Here."

"The alternative is running off to your truck and heading home. But where's the value in that, huh? You have to face it. She should too."

"I'll do it so she doesn't have to."

"Then let's go upstairs."

Terry led the way up the creaky stairwell. Adam was overpowered by the musty smell. He sneezed three times in succession.

"Y'mind? Gonna scare the ghost away."

"You could have said, *Bless you.*"

"I could've."

At the top of the stairs, Terry stopped. Adam tripped over a mechanical device on the floor.

"What the—"

"Careful with the precious merch!"

"What is this thing?" Adam asked.

"Haven't you watched our show?" Adam's blank expression told the story. "It's a sonar scanner. Detects movement using sound waves."

"Does it have to be placed in an area where someone will break their neck?"

"I wanted it to be central to the three rooms that have had activity."

"Doesn't look like it's doing anything," Adam judged.

"You'll see a lot of red on the screen if something's here."

Like a street cop directing traffic, Terry pointed at three doors of importance in the upstairs hallway.

"Door off to the left is a study. Heard a rocking sound in there two nights ago. No biggie. The door front and center, well, wait. We'll save the best for last. The door directly behind you…"

Adam turned around and glanced into a children's bedroom with mustard-colored walls. There was an unmade bunk bed and a white rocking chair in the corner of the room.

"Is the activity happening around the kids?"

"It is not. How-ever, my dog hates this room. Barks at it nonstop."

"Like a protective bark?"

"Like a foaming-at-the-mouth one."

"Oh. Where is Loomis?"

"At the hotel. He doesn't want to be near this creepfest."

Adam turned his attention back to the door that was front and center. He was already scared of what could be inside.

"The door in front of you…"

"Is that the master bedroom?" Adam asked.

"It is."

"Is that where *it* happened?"

"It is."

"I'm not going in there."

"Stand here. I'll go in."

Terry opened the door to the master bedroom slowly. Adam refused to look inside. He had his reasons.

An oak Victorian antique bed consumed most of the room's space. Other objects of note were a Persian rug, a full-length mirror, and an early 1800s French armoire.

"You see that device on the floor?" Terry asked.

Terry turned around. Adam stared at the floor.

"You don't have to go in. You just have to look at the device."

Adam glanced quickly. Terry leaned against the doorway.

"You bring an important object?"

Adam shook his head. For effect, Terry slid down the wall until his butt hit the floor. He slapped his forehead.

"That is a proximity sensor. Basically, a field of energy. If a spirit tries to penetrate it, light will flash. But a spirit only tries to penetrate it if somebody offers an object that's desirable."

"Sorry. I forgot."

"Then you, my friend, have no further reason to be here."

The front door to the home burst open. Sutton rushed through and hopped, two steps at a time, towards her father. She also tripped over the sonar scanner.

"Jesus, can everyone stop ruining my equipment?" Terry shouted.

"She replied, Dad! She saw my message, she liked it with the heart thingy, and then she decided to follow me. Isn't that great?!"

Unsure of what she was talking about, Adam nodded. Terry got the gist straight away.

"While teen crushes between two females fascinates me about as much as arranging my sock drawer, I have to inform both of you that there has been a dramatic shift in energy," Terry said dryly.

Adam tensed up. Sutton turned to her father.

"Why is that scanner thing showing a lot of red?" Sutton asked.

"It's reacting to *you*," Terry added.

"No, it's not," Sutton said.

Sutton took a step towards the master bedroom and peeked inside. She turned back to face her father and his old partner.

"Scanner doing anything now?"

Terry pointed to the scanner. The screen filled up with red.

"Keep away from that room, sweetheart," Adam advised.

"Don't call me sweetheart," Sutton said.

Sutton pretended to take a step forward. Instead, she backed into the room and grinned.

"Is she too old to be grounded?" Terry asked.

Adam altered his tone. "Sutton, I'm not kidding about this."

"As long as the door stays open, the kid'll be fine," Terry said.

Instantly, the door slammed! Adam lunged for the door handle. He jiggled the knob. Locked.

"Sutton! Are you okay?"

Even though Sutton usually dismissed anything paranormal, she had to admit that the door trick commanded her attention.

"You playing a trick on me? Terry, is this you're doing?"

"I wish I was that twisted."

"Can you open the door?"

Sutton approached the door handle. She grabbed the knob and pulled her hand back immediately.

"Ow!"

"What is it?"

"The door knob. It's hot."

Adam turned to Terry for an explanation. Terry shrugged.

"If she gets harmed, I am holding you responsible."

"If you had brought the important object, this whole process would be going a lot smoother."

Adam regretted not bringing a meaningful object from home. But he realized that his lack of preparation might not be a problem because Sutton, if she hadn't changed as much as he thought she did, could be in possession of an object that would qualify for this paranormal experiment.

"Sutton?"

"Yes...?"

"You don't happen to still wear the locket I gave you?"

"No, I don't."

This revelation deflated Adam. He couldn't expect his hormonal daughter to wear the locket he had given her about a decade ago. It wasn't hip to be wearing personal lockets in a high school universe anyway.

"I just keep it in my pocket."

Elated, Terry smacked Adam's shoulder. Adam perked up. Perhaps this locket was the key to helping his daughter. Or it could serve as the opposite since she was currently standing in the room where a notorious exorcism once occurred.

"What should she do with it?" asked Adam.

"Sutton: remove the locket from your pocket and place it in the middle of the sensor."

"How's this sensor different from the one out there?" Sutton asked.

"It's a proximity sensor. Translation: you place an object down and a light will flash if the spirit goes for it."

"Why would a spirit want this old locket?"

"We don't know that it will. Just place the locket down and tell us what happens."

Sutton removed the brass locket from her pocket, untangled the chain, and placed it in the middle of the sensor. She sat on the nearby bed. It creaked so loud she thought it would collapse to the floor.

"Object has been placed on the floor…"

"See anything yet?" Terry asked.

Adam tried the door handle again. Still locked.

"Let her be."

"If she gets harmed in any way…"

"She'll be golden. I think," Terry joked.

"You okay, Sut?"

"Yes, I'm fine. And please don't call me Sut. That's the second time today."

Adam respected her wishes and allowed a silence to creep in. Terry put his ear against the door. Sutton waited, honestly expecting nothing whatsoever to happen.

"It flashed! The light, it flashed!"

Terry howled. Adam stared at him as if to ask, "Was that completely necessary?"

"It made contact. I knew it would," Terry boasted.

"What made contact?"

"*She* did," Terry said.

Even though the answer swirled in Sutton's brain, she needed another being to validate her thought. She needed her father to validate it.

"Who did?" she asked again.

Terry elbowed Adam. Sutton waited for an answer. Adam cleared his throat before speaking.

"Your mother."

Silence swallowed up this personal moment. Adam didn't know what to say next. Even Terry didn't. Sutton shook her head in disbelief. *This was not happening*, she thought.

"Why would she want the locket you gave me, Dad?"

"Because it was from her. She made me give it you in case…something happened."

Sutton's throat tightened. She tried swallowing, but it felt like she had sharp crackers wedged in her mouth.

"Can I get a few minutes alone, please?" Sutton asked.

Adam turned to Terry to see whether or not this would be a safe idea. Terry nodded.

"We'll wait right here and we won't say a word," Adam promised.

"Can you both go outside? Or downstairs, at least?"

A minute later, Adam and Terry stepped onto the front lawn. They exchanged awkward glances.

"Will she be okay?"

"Yes."

"You swear?"

"I don't swear, but I…yeah, I firmly believe that she'll be all right."

Sutton circled the master bedroom and found discomfort in the number of times the floorboards creaked. This trip, with all of its drama and revelations from the past, unnerved her. And yet, this proximity sensor provided her with hope for the first time in years. If she only knew what to do, this moment would feel a lot less strange.

She rushed to the window, undid the lock, and raised it as high as she could.

"Dad?"

Adam whipped around and glanced at the master bedroom window. Sutton poked her head out.

"Yes, sweetheart?"

"She also told you to stop calling her that," Terry mumbled.

"Forgive me for calling you sweetheart and Sut. I'll break the habit."

"What do I say to her?"

"Whatever you want. You've seen his shows."

"She has? I knew she was a closet fan," said proudly.

Sutton shut the window. Adam stepped forward, trying to give her one last bit of advice. He held back.

"She's got this," Terry said.

In the master bedroom, Sutton thought about everything she had dreamed of asking her mother. But she knew that, whether or not she respected those that devoted their lives to investigating the paranormal, there was an art to asking spirits questions. She treaded lightly.

"Is it you, Mom?"

Nothing.

"Did something make you come back here?"

Nothing.

"Is there something you want to know about me?"

Nothing.

"I don't expect you to say anything, but maybe you could move something. Could you do that for me? Move say, the locket, to prove that you're here?"

Nothing.

"Did you give me the locket?"

Nothing.

"Was it personal to you?"

Nothing.

Sutton tired of the interrogation and considered quitting. She walked over to the door and grabbed the handle. The knob was cold.

Not only that, but it was unlocked. She could leave anytime she wanted. She took a step towards the stairwell and turned back.

"Do you miss me, Mom?"

Nothing.

Sutton became choked up. She didn't think she had the strength for the next question.

"Do you love me, Mom?"

The locket moved. Sutton covered her mouth. Tears streamed down her face. She laughed in wide-eyed wonder.

Outside, a skateboarder cruised down the sidewalk. Adam feared that the blue-haired rider would crash into his truck. At the last second, the rider swerved, hopped onto the street, and then pedaled away with his right foot. Terry ignored the rider. His full attention was on the master bedroom window.

"Um, we have a little bit of activity happening upstairs," Terry said.

Adam looked at the window of interest. It was all fogged up. A finger went up and down, forming letters. Terry squinted.

"Need my distance glasses for this," Terry stated as he ran off to his nearby van.

Adam kept his eyes glued on the finger as it finished writing. His fear evaporated the second he was able to read what the message said:

Happy Belated Birthday, Dad!

EPILOGUE

JUST A DAY LATER, the temperature had dropped thirty-five degrees. It was quite the contrast from their journey *to* Salem. All in all, Adam felt a sense of relief. He couldn't say whether Sutton had been saved, but there was a slight improvement in her attitude, tone, and body language. This, at least in his eyes, was a significant victory. He studied her in the seat; she felt his eyes on her, so she looked back at him. A smirk passed over her lips.

Sutton raised her hoodie above her head and tucked herself into a ball. This retreat reminded him of a turtle. But her gesture wasn't brought on by a desire to ignore him; she did it because she was tired.

As Sutton's energy faded away, she thought about the graphic novel she was working on and realized that, while it was a fun hobby for a girl her age, she needed to abandon it. While she was young, she wanted to have a career in paranormal investigations. She wasn't sure if her father would approve of such a path, but the trip and what happened with her deceased mother completely altered her perspective. She wished her father would get back to investigations, even if they had to take place with Terry Dennis. She was wrong about him, which begged the question: *Was she wrong about many people?*

These reflective thoughts about her future ended once she transitioned to a sleep state. While down for the so-called count, short nightmares bombarded her brain. Typically, she had nightmares with a singular focus (her last one involved a clown that ate all of her classmates' brains). But this was a different story. It was a barrage of visions that felt like constant knife pricks. She saw men and women violating zucchinis; she saw a boy wielding a knife while his mother expired on the kitchen floor; she saw a woman get trapped in a storage facility; she saw a man sitting on a couch with a violent history; she saw an elderly man in woman's attire getting stabbed repeatedly with a penknife; she saw a blushing bride leap off a hotel roof; she saw a teenage boy, not much older than herself, spread a deadly disease within the halls of his school. The visions shook her like a rickety rollercoaster, which caused her to wake up immediately.

Adam slammed on the brakes to avoid an aggressive tractor-trailer. He turned to his tired daughter, with healing arms exposed, and asked a question he prayed she would answer.

"You good?"

"Yeah."

"Promise?"

"I do."

ABOUT THE AUTHOR

E. C. Hanson earned his MFA in Dramatic Writing from NYU and was the recipient of an "Outstanding Writing For The Screen" certificate.

His work has been published by Smith & Kraus and Applause Books in 8 play anthologies. More than 35 of his short plays have been developed and produced across the United States.

Collective Tales, Curious Blue Press, Trembling With Fear, and Ghost Orchid Press intend to publish his short fiction in 2021.

As an educator, Hanson has taught undergraduate and graduate-level English courses at Sacred Heart University. He currently teaches a horror-themed writing course.

ABOUT THE EDITOR / PUBLISHER

Dawn Shea is an author and half of the publishing team over at D&T Publishing. She lives with her family in Mississippi. Always an avid horror lover, she has moved forward with her dreams of writing and publishing those things she loves so much.

D&T Previously published material:
    ABC's of Terror
    After the Kool-Aid is Gone

Follow her author page on Amazon for all publications she is featured in.
    Follow D&T Publishing at the following locations:
    Website
    Facebook: Page / Group
    Or email us here: dandtpublishing20@gmail.com

Published by D&T Publishing LLC

Cover art by Don Noble

Edited by Meghalee Mitra

Formatting by J.Z. Foster

Corinth, MS

All Things Deadly

Made in the USA
Coppell, TX
09 May 2022